# Special thanks

Allison Grier, Amber, Andrew Robinson, Anij Fallows, Anthony Kozak, Beth Barany, Bjorn Munson, Blaise Faint, Brendon Zee, Caelin Hill, Caledonia, Catherine Leja, Chad Bowden, Chris Call, Claire Ferguson-smith, CLTidball, Colleen Villasenor, Daniel Groves, Dave Baxter, Derek J. Bush, dhf, Dr. Charles Elbert Norton III, Edward Nycz Jr., Emerson Kasak, Eric Brooks, Erlinda Sustaita, Fred W Johnson, Gerald P. McDaniel, GMarkC, guardian J, Guillermo Sanchez, Heather Gearhart, Hollie Buchanan II, J. "Gwynn" Rentfleish, James Kralik. Janice Jurgens, Jared, Jeff Lewis, Jeffery Greathouse, Jennifer Johnson, Jennifer L. Pierce, Jeron Kuxhausen, John "AcesofDeath7" Mullens, John Albinsson, John Pankey, Jon, Jonathan Brown, Joshua Bowers, Joshua Chessman, Joshua Easter, Joshua McGinnis, KaS, Kelley RN, Kyle Rogers, Lisa Lyons, Lovelight Lioness Productions, Mark Newman, Mat Meillier, Matthew Johnson, Michael St. George Matatics, Michelle Marsh, Mike Connell, Monkey King Comics, Nari Muhammad, Nick Smith, Paul E. Olson, Paul Popernack, Paul Rose Jr., Paul Trinies, Paul Wocken, Philip Early, Robert Weimer, Scott Adams, Scott Kilburn, Sean Brislen, Sean Iffland, Shannon Carlin, Stabbath, Stephen, Taiga Char, Tom S, Victoria Nohelty, Vince, Vulpecula, Walter Weiss, and Weasel.

# Also by Russell Nohelty

**THE OBSIDIAN SPINDLE SAGA**
The Sleeping Beauty
The Wicked Witch
The Fairy Queen
The Red Rider
**THE GODVERSE CHRONICLES**
And Death Followed Behind Her
And Doom Followed Behind Her
And Ruin Followed Behind Her
And Hell Followed Behind Her
And Conquest Followed Behind Them
And Darkness Followed Behind Her
And Chaos Followed Behind Them
Katrina Hates the Dead
Pixie Dust
**OTHER NOVEL WORK**
My Father Didn't Kill Himself
Sorry for Existing
Gumshoes: The Case of Madison's Father
The Invasion Saga
The Vessel
Worst Thing in the Universe
The Void Calls Us Home
The Marked Ones
**OTHER ILLUSTRATED WORK**
The Little Bird and the Little Worm
Ichabod Jones: Monster Hunter
Gherkin Boy
**www.russellnohelty.com**

# The Dragon Scourge

## Book 1 of Dragon Strife

By:

Russell Nohelty

Edited by:

Lily Luchesi

Proofread by:

Katrina Roets

Cover by:

Paramita Bhattacharjee

# Chapter 1

Today, I will die.

This wasn't a surprise to me. I had been preparing for it my whole life, but I never thought it would come until it crashed upon me this morning like a suffocating wave. Fifteen years on this Earth seemed like so much time when I was younger, but now, at the end, I realized how little time it really was.

I was always an early bird. I woke with the sun, ready for the start of a new day. However, when the tender kiss of light touched my eyes on my final morning alive, I shut them tighter and pulled my sheets over my head. If I didn't face the day, then perhaps my death would never come.

I trained for this since I was a small child, but there is no amount of preparation that readied you for being swallowed by a dragon; its horrible, jagged teeth ripping through the white dress Sister Milka sewed special for the occasion and tearing your flesh as it gnashed against your virgin body.

Somebody softly knocked on the door to my room. "Gilda, we need to get started. Today is a big day."

Sacrifices were given every privilege. We wanted for nothing in our short lives, and after our deaths, those we loved were taken care of for the rest of their days. It was what the villagers bestowed upon us to assuage their guilt, and it was a small price to pay compared to the one we paid.

We were the salvation of the village, after all. It was only because of our noble sacrifice that the great dragon lord Ewig stayed satiated in his cave inside the volcano that loomed above us and didn't sweep down to destroy us.

That was the pact, cemented in blood a hundred years ago. Every five years, one of us must willingly walk to our deaths, and in return, the great dragon would watch over our village, and prevent the great volcano that loomed over us from erupting, burying our village under its magma.

It was a great honor to be chosen as the sacrificial lamb. That was what the line they told me at least, but today it certainly didn't seem like an honor. It seemed like I was raised like a lamb for slaughter, provided every luxury to die at the right moment.

"Coming!" I said after a long pause. Sister Milka was a harsh and unforgiving mistress, and would not accept anything but perfection today, on my last day of life. Every day of my life she watched over me, training me to die well. Even now, at the end, she would not take her foot off my neck. Especially now, with so much on the line, with the prosperity of our town riding on the spillage of my blood before the clock struck midnight tonight.

I slipped my sandals on my feet and rose to stand. Before I answered the door, I spun and made my bed, as I was trained to do; the first sign of an uncluttered mind was a perfectly made bed. It was the least we could do to show how much we appreciated all we were given.

As I pulled the corner of the bed taut, I thought about not tucking in the final edge as a little sign of rebellion. However, when I tried to leave it mussed, pangs of guilt washed over me, until they were so overwhelming that, with shaking hands, I forced the last edge of my blanket in tightly.

Once I was dead, my house would become a museum, and my room a shrine, preserved exactly how I left it, and I didn't want my mother to have to explain that her perfect daughter died a slob. *Why do I care what people think of me after my death?*

With the bed made, I walked to the door and placed my hand on the knob. The minute I opened it, the machinations of my last hours, those that I trained for my whole life, would wash over me one after another.

"It's time to open this door, missy."

I closed my eyes and felt my breath against my chest, rising and lowering in slow, rhythmic time with the beating of my heart. They were small gestures, in the grand scheme, but right now, they were everything, and soon, much too soon, they would fall fallow and motionless forever.

What would happen after I took my final breath? According to the church, I would rise up into the sky and take my place among the stars, but what did they know? The gods were long dead, and the dragons that remained had none of their love of humanity.

Banging came from the other side of the door, and Sister Milka's shrill voice cut through the air. "That's quite enough of this dawdling, Gilda! Open the door this instant."

Her shouting pulled me out of my calm, and I turned the doorknob. She exploded into the room, her trim frame and long face cutting an imposing image against the harsh light that fell into the room. She was not a big woman, but her presence filled my small room like none other.

"Good morning, mistress," I said, bowing my head to avoid her gaze. You never looked the nuns in the eyes.

She didn't answer for a long moment, busying herself with checking my room, inspecting my bed, and running her fingers across the top of my dresser, looking for dust. She rubbed her fingers together and gave a small nod. "I see your mother took this cleaning seriously."

I nodded to her, keeping my eyes turned to the ground. "Of course, mistress. She scrubbed all day and into the evening."

Sister Milka not only ran the monastery and school in town, but personally looked over all of us chosen for sacrifice, of which there were three at any time. It was a job she took seriously and had since taking her vows fifty years ago.

"Well, let me get a look at you," she said. "Stand up straight."

It was crucial that I not have a flaw or imperfection on my naked body, and for fifteen years I can't remember a time when I lifted a finger in manual labor. My mother made all my meals, or a member of the community would deliver it, and everything else was taken care of so I could keep myself flawless for my date with Ewig.

I dropped my nightgown to the floor and endured the intense gaze of Sister Milka as she examined every inch of me. Two years ago, I judged a livestock competition, and she looked at me like the other judges looked at the cattle on display, trying to decide which one would give the best meat.

"You need to shave every inch of you, except your head," she said. "We do not want the great dragon lord to get a hairball now, do we?"

I shook my head. "No, mistress."

"Good, good." She placed her hands under my breasts, and then pinched the sides of my waist. "You have put on decent weight in the past year, my dear. Yes, I think the dragon lord will be most impressed with you." Then she moved her hand to my face, and brushed her hand along my cheek. "You are truly one of my greatest girls. I am so proud of what you have become."

*A compliment?* She never gave me a compliment before. She had nothing but bitter, terse words for me, that stuck into my gut with pain and tore at my mind.

"T-thank you, mistress."

She moved her hand to my chin and pulled it up to meet her eyes, a great honor she afforded very few. "No, thank you, my dear. The sacrifice you make tonight is a greater burden than any child should bear."

Tears filled my eyes as I stared into Sister Milka's face. Her eyes were a cold, dark brown, and even though her words were kind, her face was sharp, and her voice terse, taking much of the tenderness from them.

"No need for that." Sister Milka pulled her hand from my face and slid a white handkerchief from her pocket. "This is a happy occasion, after all. Your sacrifice will save us all. There is no greater gift. Now, clean yourself up, and I will draw your bath."

# Chapter 2

Every morning, I soaked in a tub of buttermilk and rose petals for one hour. A small fire pit under the porcelain tub heated the buttermilk, so it would soak into my skin better, making it satin smooth. It wasn't until this morning that I realized it also helped make me taste delicious to the great dragon who would consume me later in the day, like a hunk of stew meat marinated overnight for a great feast. Like the one we would have tonight in my honor, the one time in the last five years everyone in the town would eat as well as I did every night.

Even with Ewig's blessing, my village was a harsh place to live, even in the best of times. The land was unyielding, and it took hardened souls to work it. Children were raised from a young age for a hard life in the fields or cutting timber in the forest. Time chiseled our jaws and hardened our bodies until our palms were little more than one large callus.

Not me, though. My hands were as smooth as a newborn's, and my face never lost its baby fat. While my classmates wanted for food all the time and their stomachs cried out for even a sliver of a morsel, my belly was always full. Fifteen years of a full belly in exchange for my life seemed like a worse deal the older I became, but it was a good way to live.

"Don't forget to scrub off the dead flesh," Sister Milka said from the other room. "Nothing but the newest, freshest skin for Ewig's feast."

The hardest part of my day was pumicing the dead skin off my arms and legs. When I was done, my legs were red and raw, and after I shaved, my body was smooth and hairless, except for the three-foot long hair on top of my head. After an hour, I stood and stepped out of the tub, dripping myself dry as I wiped the fogged mirror on the far side of the room. My face was round, and the freckles on either side of my cheeks popped against my pale, ivory skin. I was not allowed in the light of the sun, and if I needed to step outside during the day, a parasol was absolutely essential so as to not spoil Ewig's prize.

I touched my cheek, feeling the fresh, smooth skin underneath it, and longed for a long life of hardship, like the others in my village, instead of a short life of decadence like I had lived for far too short a time.

I received jealous looks whenever others had to sacrifice their rations to me during a famine, or a drought, but Sister Milka was quick to point out that I would burn bright and fast, then extinguish brilliantly in order to save them all. Compared to that, any other sacrifice was inconsequential. All that mattered was keeping me and the other girls safe so that the village may live on in prosperity.

I wondered often, as they glowered at me, how many of them would trade places with me if they could. It was impolite to ask, but if I

mustered the courage, and they were honest with their answers, I wondered what they would say. Could they even understand what it meant to live my life, to know without a doubt that you would never live to graduate, get married, or have a child? My life was full of frivolities, yes, and I was granted access to a level of wealth that I could never hope to achieve on my own, but that access came at the price of my life.

"One hundred brushes for every strand," Sister Milka said from the other room. "I will know if you have slacked off."

What did it matter if I brushed my hair a hundred times, or twenty? Would the others hold it against me when I would be dead by the next sunrise? Would Ewig refuse to rip me apart if I chose to stow my brush, or if I cut my hair in the short bob I always coveted on the other girls in class?

"Yes, mistress," I said.

No, it didn't matter what I did, I was sure of it. Ewig would eat me either way. This part wasn't about me. It was about Sister Milka, who would return to the village after escorting me to the entrance of Ewig's cave, tears in her eyes, and give a final blessing to those gathered at the edge of town; the mayor, the elders of the town, the soldiers who would report back to the king of our success, the other cedars who would sacrifice their lives in due time, and my mother.

This was about her appearance, as the elders gathered around and praised her fortitude, patting her on the back for raising such a strong

sacrifice. She was such a powerful force in town because she knew how to put on a performance and gain the approval of those in power.

As I ran the brush through my long, straight hair, I counted to myself. I had never been able to cut it even once in my whole life. Gods forbid the hairdresser accidentally nicked me with the scissors, and spoiled Ewig's great prize.

*1, 2, 3...*

The vanity where I sat had a mirror perched atop it, an ivory thing with gold-inlaid, worth more than Mama could hope to earn in three lifetimes as a tailor, and yet, its opulence was matched by every piece in the room, all delicate enough to break with the slightest touch, which made them all the more valuable.

I couldn't help but feel as delicate as the mirror that reflected my white skin back to me. We were the same shade of alabaster, and neither had lived much life outside of the walls of my room. However, it would continue on, entombed in this bathroom, for a hundred years or more, while I would be dead when the sun dipped below the horizon.

*12, 13, 14...*

It was a silly little thing, having grown up as a sacrifice my whole life, but I never thought this day was coming. Nobody ever thought they were going to die, and yet here I was, preparing for my willing demise. *Why are you so pathetic that you would allow them to kill you without a fight?*

The tears came, and I swallowed them back. This was my duty to the town, to my mother, to myself. So few have a great destiny, who was I to deny mine? "Try not to think about it, Gilda," I said with a calming breath. "Lose yourself in the counting, as you do every other morning."

*24, 25, 25, 27...*

It will all be over soon. It will all be done, and there will be nothing left but the great beyond, and the eternal reward of never-ending non-existence, and never having to worry about another thing ever again.

*Won't that be nice?*

# Chapter 3

After brushing my hair, I had to present myself naked to Sister Milka before getting dressed. She walked into the bathroom and ran her knobby knuckles through my hair. If I had even one knot, she would make me do everything again, one hundred brushes for each strand of hair.

This morning I must have pleased her, because she looked at me through the mirror with delicate eyes and squeezed my shoulders tightly. "You have become quite a woman."

I smiled at her, trying hard not to spew the venom that filled my mouth. "That's very kind."

*I'm not going to become a woman.* That's what I wanted to say as I grabbed the vanity and smashed her over the head with it. The thought of it brought a small smile to my face, which she must have taken as appreciation for her kindness, instead of exhilaration at the fleeting image of her death at my hand, but I could never do that. I was a good girl after all, who dutifully did as she was told.

I clenched my fist tightly as she pulled my arms to stand and guided me by the small of my back into the other room. I absolutely hated the liberty she took touching my body, but there was nothing to be done about it. I had none of the power here. If I did, then I certainly wouldn't be walking to my death tonight.

"Now, state the cedar's creed," she said.

The cedar's creed was the reason we did what we did. It was the recitation of the reason behind everything.

"Every five years, the Dragon Lord Ewig must be appeased with a sacrifice to renew his pact with his chosen people. I have been chosen to fulfill a great purpose, to act as kindling on the pyre of our love for him."

It was our mantra, and Sister Milka made us say it a dozen times a day.

"Good," Sister Milka said. "Now, the compact."

I nodded. "Great dragon Ewig, I offer myself to you, for the protection of my people, as payment for your grace and your love. For your fealty, I offer my blood, as a symbol of the bond between your chosen people and your grace. As it washes down your throat, remember your oath to them. I offer my flesh, as remembrance of the protection your countenance provides from the looming volcano threat that has long plagued us. As it coats your tongue, allow our pact to be renewed for another half a decade, and know all we do is in service to your glory. I offer my soul to you, complete and unmolested. As it touches every inch of you, know that we are powerless in your company, and look to you to light the way for us."

I had said those words every morning since I could remember, and before I could speak, they were recited to me, until they had bored into the base of my brain. They used to give me pause, and some days I would cry as I stuttered over them, thinking of my flesh being torn from my body and my soul being enveloped in the dragon's flame.

Now, they came out of my mouth with droll, rote emotion.

"Very good," Sister Milka said with as much enthusiasm as I gave to her. "Now, remember, in the moment, when the great eye of Ewig falls on you, summon all your courage, and your training, to say the verses perfectly."

"And what will happen if I don't, sister?" I asked. It was something I thought about these last long, hard months, but never had the strength to push out of my mouth. "Will he not devour me if I don't speak flawlessly?"

"What he does to you is not my concern," Sister Milka said. "My concern is for the village, and in order to renew our pact with the great dragon, the words are as important as the vessel. They must be spoken impeccably."

*I was not her concern.* That much had been clear for a long time now. Years ago, when I was young, I thought Sister Milka was a friend. I once considered her family. It wasn't until I grew into my role, and truly understood it backwards and forwards, that I realized that she was not on my side. Her job was to teach me how to die well; to fulfill my duty without question; to pound me into submission so I would not run under any circumstances.

"Gilda!" my mother shouted from the other room. I heard her loud steps down the hall, and she opened the creaky door. "Breakfast."

My mother never wanted to sacrifice me. That much she made clear as often as possible, but she still accepted the gifts the elders bestowed on her. She did not steal me away in the night. She did not rail against my fate, nor would she do so today, on my last day of life.

"We haven't finished yet, Odine," Sister Milka said. "We have much to discuss. This is a very important day, after all. Leave us to it."

My mother was a stout woman, with a round face and eyes like coal that burned with rage as they caught Sister Milka's gaze, unafraid of the consequence borne of doing so.

Most women wore tanned dresses of dark brown that mixed with the mud and grime of the village during a rainstorm, but she wore bright colors, embroidered with flowers and jewels. Color was a sign of wealth, and if she was going to give her daughter away as the virginal sacrifice to the great dragon inside the mountain, she would not fade quietly into the darkness.

This morning, she covered the green dress with a red and white checkered apron, and when she smiled a curt smile, the dimples on each side of her face cut deep grooves in her cheeks.

"I think she's studied enough for one lifetime," Mom said.

"That is not your choice, Odine," Sister Milka said, her voice growing deeper, and more authoritative, with each word. "The church ha—"

"This is my daughter's last day," Mom said. "And I made all her favorites. We will sit down as a family, her and I, and you will leave so that we might enjoy a final meal together before the eyes of the town fall on her. I think I've entertained you quite enough for one lifetime."

Sister Milka growled, darting her eyes between us, before she sighed. "Very well. I suppose she is as ready as we will ever be." She turned to me. "You have a ten o'clock meeting with the mayor, and the tailor will be here in thirty minutes to fit you with your dress for this evening. Do not eat so much that you cannot fit into it."

"Hey!" my mother said. "If she wants to eat until she bursts, that's her right today, especially today of all days."

"Quite." Sister Milka turned to the door. "See that she doesn't burst, Odine. She must make it to her betrothed."

My mother's voice vibrated and cracked as the tears filled her eyes. "Don't tell me what to do, Sister. I have just about lost my patience with you."

Sister Milka smirked at her. "Have a good day, Odine."

Without another word, she slid out the door and slithered down the hall, her long black dress swishing against the wood floors.

"Come on now," Mom said. "Get dressed and then come to breakfast."

I stood and walked to my dresser. "Did you really make my favorites?"

"Of course, my sweet baby," she replied. The tears streamed down either side of her red-cheeked face. "It's your special day."

# Chapter 4

The cedar sacrifice was always the first girl born after the previous sacrifice was given to the great dragon lord. It could have been any child in the village if they were born on the right day and the right gender, but it ended up being me. My best friend Leyhan could have been chosen if he had been a girl. He was born three weeks before me, but he was a man, and thus disqualified from being a sacrifice.

That fate fell to me. I was happy that at least nobody else had to go to their death. If it was anyone, I was glad fate chose me.

And I know, I know it wasn't my mother's fault, but it was sometimes hard not to put the blame on her...and my father, wherever he ended up after abandoning us. If he was still around, I would have shifted some of the blame to him, but he vanished without a trace when I was a toddler, leaving my mother to raise me alone.

"It smells good," I said, walking gingerly into the kitchen.

Mom was still busying herself in the kitchen, bringing bacon and bagels to the table as I slid into the wood chair where I had eaten almost every meal of my small, pathetic life.

The table was chockablock full of pancakes and waffles, along with milk, and apple juice.

The salty smell of sizzling bacon filled my nose as she slid a plate onto the argyle tablecloth, only to be overwhelmed by sausage links in the next second.

"You didn't have to do all this, Mom."

She sat down across from me. Her eyes were puffy and red. "I couldn't sleep. I have been up for hours."

"I couldn't sleep either."

"That's a shame," she said. "You've always been a good sleeper, and I was hoping—" She choked on her own words and used her napkin to blot her eyes. "—I was hoping you would have one more peaceful night."

"Every night will be peaceful after tonight," I replied to her lowly, swallowing the truth of my words.

She wept for me, but not once did she try to steal me away in the middle of the night, and even now, at the end, I didn't see a suitcase packed by the heavy oak doors. She was just going to let it happen, and for that, I did blame her. However, I swallowed my anger lest it turned to guilt. She would have a hard enough time living with herself after tonight, and that was her burden. Dying well was mine.

I stacked my plate up high with pancakes drizzled in syrup and steeped in butter. I tossed bacon and sausages on my pile of food and allowed them to stew in the sweetness.

"Did I ever tell you why your father left?" she asked after staying silent for a long while.

I shook my head. "No, never."

She swallowed the lump in her throat. "After your birth, when you were consecrated as the next sacrifice—your father didn't handle it well. He begged for them to choose another, but this was tradition, and the town elders were powerless to change it."

"No, they could have changed it," I replied. "They just didn't. And if they did, they would have taken another child. I don't want that."

She held up her hand. "Please, this is hard enough to get through."

"Sorry."

She took a long sip of her coffee. "No, I'm sorry. You have nothing to apologize for. I shouldn't have—it's just I really want to tell you this story. You deserve to know it, before the end."

I nodded as I bit off a bit of bacon. "Then please, continue."

"Thank you." She sighed. "The elders denying your father's request wasn't the end of it. He was determined to keep you alive. He planned to steal you in the middle of the night, off into the woods, to live among the trees."

"He did?" I asked. "And what did you do?"

"I—I—" She stuttered and stammered. "Oh gods, this is so hard—I told him no. I didn't know how we would survive in the woods. I couldn't forage and he couldn't hunt, but he swore it would be okay. I thought it was a fool's dream, something to keep him occupied, but in the end, a fruitless one, that would fade with time."

"It didn't, though?"

She shook her head. "No, it didn't. Even once we moved into this house, and the trappings of opulence surrounded us, he kept going, plotting and planning, until he was ready." She dabbed her cheeks with a cloth napkin. "He was very convincing, your father, and eventually he even got me believing that we could make it. He told me there was a town thirty miles west that needed a tailor and a cobbler. We were both good artisans, even though it had been years since we touched our tools—it was a fool's dream, what he had."

I had stopped eating and leaned in to catch every word. "What happened?"

"He trusted the wrong person."

"Who?" I asked. "Who betrayed him?"

She blinked, and again, but no words came from her mouth for a long time. "...Me."

I dropped the fork, and it clinked against the plate on the table. "...You?"

"You have to understand. What he was asking..."

My teeth ground against themselves as I tried to hold in my anger. "My father tried to save me, and you—you stopped him!" I stood. "Why did you doom me to this life?"

"It—it wasn't completely me. Your father was sloppy, and careless. He was going out at all hours of the night, and stockpiling—the mayor brought me to his house, and asked me in front of the town elders, and in the light of the great dragon's visage, if my father planned to betray them."

"And you told them the *truth*?"

"What was I going to do? If I kept his secret, you would have been taken from me. If he stole you away, then they would have chosen another to sacrifice. Would you rather your friend be chosen? I could not ask anyone else to bear the burden of losing their child, no matter how much it pained me."

"Then you would rather I die?"

"I would rather we bore this burden than another."

"Thank you for making that decision for me."

"Would you have made a different one?"

I began to speak, but I stopped. She was right, after all. I would rather deal with it than some other child. If it was my burden to bear, then nobody else would have to deal with it.

"This is terrible," I said.

"Rightly, so." She sighed. "They placated me with the finest riches, but I always saw them as trappings of a life that I chose over my own child, and I'm sorry for that. I'm so so so so sorry."

I knew she wanted absolution, but I couldn't give it to her. "What happened to Dad?"

Her eyes narrowed. "They were merciful. They let him live but exiled him to the outer reaches of the forest. I think they wanted him to live with the idea that he failed, and his daughter was doomed. It's a guilt I live with every day, and it has nearly killed me. Every time I hear the rustle of the trees, I think he might be back for you." Her eyes met mine. "I don't know how I'm going to go on without you."

"No," I replied quickly and curtly. "You don't get to be the one who feels bad today. You don't get to put this on me, when you could have stopped it. Parents are supposed to protect their children, not let them become dragon fodder."

She sighed. "You're right."

"But if you need a reason to continue, do it so that every time you walk down the street, every person remembers the sacrifice you made—that I made. Rub it in their face as much as possible. Do not cower as the other families have, retreating into themselves. Live, and make my death matter."

Mom shook her head. "I don't know if I can do that."

"I don't care," I replied. "This isn't about you."

There was a knock on the door, and I went to answer it. I was so angry with my mother, I didn't want to look at her for another minute, and I was angry with myself, because even with her confession, I didn't hate her. I almost empathized with her, even in my seething bitterness.

When I opened the door, Seamus, the kindly, old tailor who made every sacrificial dress after my mother stopped working as one, stood in front of me, white-haired, with a long goatee, and wrapped around with a long tape measure. In his hand he held a long lace dress that I recognized immediately. It was the one I would die in, and the last thing I would ever wear.

"Good morrow, Miss Gilda." His smile beamed across his face, making his eyes little more than slits. "I come for your final fitting."

No, he wasn't actually kind at all, was he? He was polite and gentle, but he wasn't kind. A kind person wouldn't be party to such a tragedy as my death. In that way, there wasn't a kind person in this whole village. They had driven the only kind person away when they exiled my father, and I would never forgive them for it. Luckily for them, my grudge would only last for one more night, until the dragon's fire consumed me.

"Of course," I replied. "Please, come in."

# Chapter 5

*Cedars.* That's what they call us, not sacrifices, like the trees that line our woods. We are kindling, an inanimate thing that brings warmth to others.

Sister Milka returned in the middle of my fitting, entering the room when I was standing in the lace dress I would die in.

"My gods," she uttered after gasping in astonishment. "Aren't you a vision?"

I looked at myself in the full-length mirror that I stood in front of, propped up on an apple box so that the tailor could work on the hem of my dress, which was a half inch too long, and dragged along the ground. Gods forbid I muss it up along the dirt path from my house to the mountain.

"I suppose so," I replied.

I pulled my long hair behind my ear and looked at myself, really looked at myself, as I am not usually wont to do. The light coming in from the window illuminated my dress, and the sequins on the bustle shimmered like the night sky. This was how I pictured I would look on my wedding dress, something I would never have. Sister Milka tried to convince me that I had been betrothed to Ewig at birth, and tonight I would be his bloody bride, but husbands did not kill their wives.

Sister Milka looked along the room to the cuckoo clock hanging on the wall next to the mirror.

"My lords, is that the time?" She looked down at the tailor. "Seamus, are you quite done?"

"Almost, mum," Seamus replied.

"You have two minutes. Otherwise, we will be late, and we have precious little free minutes today. There is a schedule to keep."

Gods forbid we miss our next appointment. That would look poorly on Sister Milka, and, for her, appearance was everything. If she couldn't even claim the illusion of perfection, then what was left of her poor, miserable life?

Seamus placed one more pin that came dreadfully close to pricking my ankle and turned to Sister Milka. "There we go. She's plumped out nicely. The dragon lord will be pleased with her."

"I should hope so." Sister Milka walked forward. "She was such a ruddy little thing when we first met. I never thought she would mature but look at her now."

They talked about me as if I wasn't in the room. Dissociation was normal for everyone in town, though, so I was used to it. If they actually saw me as a person—a living breathing thing—then it became harder to let me walk to my death. I hated to say it, but I did the same with the other sacrifices. Now I know how lonely it was to be me right now, misunderstood by the willfully ignorant.

"Well, don't just sit there." Sister Milka clapped her hands. "Change so Seamus can make his last alterations. The children will be waiting."

It was tradition for the sacrifice to ring the morning bell at school, and then read a story to the children, before having them offer a final prayer to the cedar. I had watched others do it twice before, and now it was my turn.

I pulled off the fine lace dress and slipped into a thick cotton one, the same color white as the one I had taken off. While my mother had the freedom to wear just about any color, white was reserved for brides and sacrifices, with us being the only who could wear it outside of their wedding day.

"Do keep up," Sister Milka said as we walked across the square in the middle of town. Usually, the grass was empty, but for the past week they had been setting up for tonight's feast. Once every five years, every citizen, no matter how rich or poor, sat at the same table and stuffed themselves on the finest meats and cheeses, as one of us went to our deaths.

"Yes, mum."

The Feast of the Cedars, it was called. A remembrance of those who died before in sacrifice to the great dragon Ewig, and in celebration of the most recent cedar. The only time the town willingly thought of those that died so they could live. Tonight, that would be me.

"Oh, isn't it beautiful, Gilda?" Sister Milka said, reveling in the delicate snowflakes hung all around the square. "They are really going to send you off in style."

"It's lovely," I replied, stifling my emotions. I didn't see beauty in the decorations. I only saw death. "But we must not dawdle, sister."

She nodded. "Of course."

The school sat on the other end of the square from the small stone church, and were the two tallest buildings in town, as they were the only that were allowed steeples, for the bells that sat in their belfries.

As we passed the stage at the head of the feast, where I would sit along with Sister Milka and the village elders, providing one last spectacle for the gathered masses to gawk at and offer their condolences, I heard the playful sounds of schoolchildren laughing.

The school was a small thing, with only one classroom that housed all the children, and the nuns taught all of us as one. I had gone through fifth grade, but once I turned eleven Sister Milka removed me from school altogether, as there was no use wasting a seat on somebody who wouldn't apprentice for one of the local shops in town. From then on, she tutored me exclusively.

The school gave a base of knowledge for all students before they went into a specialty trade and apprenticed under one of the artisans in town. Then, it acted as a daycare for those apprenticeships when the students were not needed, or when the shop was closed. Since the only thing I had to look forward to was death, there was no need for me to apprentice under anyone. It would be a waste of precious resources.

When I stepped onto the dirt street in front of the school and the children got a look at me, all the playful energy stopped. All the eyes followed me as I walked up the stairs to the front door, where another nun stood with a thick rope.

Even the nun's face dropped when she saw me, though they recovered quickly. Though I was always treated as apart from the rest of the villagers, as a thing to them instead of a person, it was hard to deny on this of all days that they were sacrificing one of their own.

"Good morrow, sister." The nun handed the rope to Sister Milka. "May the lords be with you."

"And with you." Sister Milka turned to me and held out the rope. "Not too hard. You would hate to blister your perfect fingers on your big day."

I took the rope in my hand. It was coarse and rough. As I wrapped my fingers around it, the frayed edges pinched at my delicate skin. I pulled the rope down, and the bell began to ring. The sound seemed enough to knock the children out of their haze, and they marched dutifully into the room.

As they passed, my eyes tracked, trying to find Leyhan, but didn't find him among the crowd. Leyhan must have been needed at the bakery, because he would never intentionally miss such an important day.

A little girl with blonde hair, nearly five to the day, beelined right toward me after the other students had made their way inside. Her white dress stood out against the black and gray of the other uniforms. Bella had been named a sacrifice a day after the previous ceremony. She had crisp blue eyes and curly blonde hair that was impossible to tame, even after a hundred brushes every morning and night.

"Good morrow, Bella," I said with a smile. "And how are you today?"

She opened her mouth to say something, but only a shriek emerged as she wrapped her hands around me and buried her head in my dress.

"It's a tough day for her." From around the corner, another white dress emerged. Unlike Bella, or even myself, Thorna's hair was jet black, and her face was gaunt. She had five years to plump herself up for the dragon lord, and yet, every time I saw her, she seemed thinner and leaner.

"Now, now," Sister Milka said, trying to pull Bella off me. "That is no way to behave."

"No!" Bella shouted, refusing to give up an inch.

"It's okay, sister," I said after a fruitless struggle between them. "I'll clean her up and bring her inside."

"See that you do it quickly." Sister Milka replied. "We have tea with the mayor in an hour." She turned to Thorna and sneered. "Bring her inside, too, and see if you can talk some sense into her."

"I will."

# Chapter 6

"I can't believe you're going through with this," Thorna said as the three of us sat on the steps of the school. It had taken me five minutes to coax Bella off my leg and only after I convinced Thorna to come out of her perch and join us.

If any of the other students had failed to show up on time for school, they would have been lashed a half dozen times, until the backs of their uniforms were stained with blood. However, one of the privileges of being a cedar was that we could skirt many of the town's laws, within reason and sometimes outside of it. Thorna had become a master at pushing the boundaries of what was acceptable in her short ten years on this Earth. I wished I had half her strength.

"I don't have much of a choice," I replied.

There was a special bond between cedars. Thorna and Bella were the only two people in the whole world who could understand how I felt, and it was the same for me. To have a horrible fate thrust on you with no way to change it was a future I didn't wish on anyone, but I appreciated that at least these two knew my pain, and were there to comfort me, just as I had for those before me. When I was their ages, I bonded with Freja and Renata, the two cedars before me, who went to their death with grace and equanimity befitting nobility. There was a chain that stretched back a hundred years, and we cedars were all linked to it.

"Sure you do," Thorna said. "You could run. You could hide. You could fight."

"And then what? I would be found sooner or later, and we would be in the same place as we are now."

"Or they would cut you down in the square," Bella said. I hated that she knew about such cruelty at a young age, but the consequences of running were drilled into us early. "But only after they kill everyone you ever loved."

That meant my mother. Before this morning, it was enough to keep me in line and now, even though she betrayed me, I didn't want her to die because of my impetuousness.

"That's why I don't have anybody I love," Thorna said. "It makes things too complicated."

"Then you still mean to run?" I said.

She nodded. "Just need to find the right time. Gonna take Bella with me."

Bella shook her head. "No, I'm not going. I want to be brave, like Gilda."

I mussed her long hair, uncut just like mine and Thorna's, but much shorter. "I don't know if what I'm doing is brave. It feels...easy. Like the whole of the universe is pushing me in one direction, and it would be too hard to swim the other way."

"That is some straight-up, brain-washed patriarchy garbage," Thorna said. "Did you know three boys were born before me? Were they even considered as cedars? Of course not, because the sacrifice must be a virginal girl. That's why I'm leaving all this behind. Screw this stupid town, my stupid family, and this whole stupid life."

I looked into Thorna's eyes. "I hope you make it."

It occurred to me how old Freja looked when she went to her death. I thought she was the wisest person in the whole world, and Bella looked at me that way now. Renata didn't look quite as old when she was sacrificed five years ago, but they both seemed to be the most mature people in the whole world. Now, I knew the truth. They were just scared little girls, like me, who didn't know how to escape the fate thrust upon them.

"I hope you don't," Thorna said with a scoff. "I hope you trip and fall down that mountain, and wind up at the bottom, alive and alone, with no other option but to run."

"If that happens, then it would only upset the great dragon lord, and he would wreak his vengeance on this whole town, including you. He would abandon the volcano and let it engulf this whole town in flames."

"Good," Thorna replied.

"He will burn everyone, including you and Bella."

"Then I'll offer myself up if he comes," Bella said, full of vim and confidence. "I ain't scared of him."

"No," I said. "I guess you aren't, are you?" I moved my eyes between them. "I wish I was half as wonderful as you when I was your age."

"Gilda!" Sister Milka shouted from inside. "Bring the girls inside. It's time for a story."

"You don't have to listen to them," Thorna said. "This is your last day on Earth. At least you shouldn't have to take orders today."

I winced as I stood, trying to force a smile. "Yes, I do. When you reach the time of your ceding, you can make another choice, but I have made mine." I reached down to help Bella up. "Come now, dear. Let me tell you a story."

"I like stories," Bella said with a smile as she walked with me into the school. Thorna gave a resigned growl, and then stomped into the room after me. While she didn't like my choice, at least she agreed it was mine to make, in a world where every decision was made for me.

The school room was just as I remembered it and carried the musk of sweat and dirt. The children sat at long benches, and all turned to me as I entered. Thorna found a spot at the back of the room, but Bella refused to let me go, even when I was at the front of the room.

"The children have chosen," Sister Milka said, handing me a small hymnal book I had read a hundred times before. "Today we read *The Great*

*Lord Ewig's Gift,* by our town's most important founder, Yesibel Onshure."

I hated that book. I was forced to read it a hundred times in my life, and it was the last thing I wanted to do today, but today wasn't about me. Not really. It was about the townspeople, and them feeling like they sent me off with honor, even if I felt no honor in how I was being led to slaughter.

I caught eyes with Thorna in the back of the room, and her face was filled with disappointment. She would thrash and fight every step of the way to the gallows. She would have to be hogtied before she gave her life for a town that waited to kill her. For a moment I wished I could be that selfish, but then that desire vanished, and I smiled at the class.

I grabbed the book from Sister Milka and pulled Bella up on my lap. "What do you think? Do you want to hear about how the great dragon Ewig saved us all?"

"Yeah!" the group shouted, except for Bella and Thorna, who turned away in disgust. However, Bella still held firm to my stomach, refusing to let go.

"Very well," I replied, opening the page. "'Once upon a time, the great dragon lords finished their battle with the gods and came out victorious. The twelve lords, having proved themselves greater than even the divinities, each claimed a piece of the new world for themselves. Ramidion, the greatest of the lords, settled in the center of the land, in the Capitol, claiming the most fertile land for herself. Virtri, the wisest of the lords, settled in the north, surrounded by the largest library in the world. Qyghem, the most pious of the dragon lords, took his leave in the east, founding a great monastery devoted to the church of the dragon lords. It went on like that for all of the brothers and sisters, each cutting a swath of Ashceles and staking their claim to it.

"'When it came to Ewig, the youngest and most cunning of the dragon lords, he did not choose the flashiest place to call his own, or the most fruitful, or the most powerful. He knew that those lands would be beset with conquerors and war. Instead, he chose the most peaceful place he could find, nestled in the furthest corner of the land, untouched by the horrible wars that plagued our great land.

"'All of the dragon lords made one request for their part in saving humanity from the gods that wished to destroy them. A single child, fifteen and virginal, as a sacrifice to their greatness, on the vernal equinox of every fifth rotation of the sun. In return, they would bestow on us their countenance. Ewig, for his grace, offered his protection from the great volcano that plagued our land, and a safe haven in the dark forest, in return for his sacrifice.'"

I stopped, trying to contain the tears that streamed down my face. "'It was an impossible choice for those of us that wandered to settle in the new city, free from the harsh conditions of the rest of the forest, but we came anyway, and then, five years hence, we convened for the first ceding. The people fought among each other, protecting their own, for hours, until I, Yesibel Onshure, stepped forward and offered my daughter as the first sacrifice, pleasing the great lord, and horrifying all in my presence. However, I could not ask them to do something I myself was not willing to do.'"

I choked on my tears. "'The great dragon was pleased, and in return for our sacrifice, he promised to rain down his beneficence upon us. Since then, our land has grown strong, free of war, pestilence, and plague. It is a hard life, but a safe one, in the shadow of the dragon. Glory be to the good lord Ewig.'"

My lip quivered as I ended the story. Bella wasn't any help, as I heard her sniffling as she burrowed into my shoulder. It took me a moment to recover, but after I wiped my eyes, I stood up and took a deep breath. Bella still clung to me.

"Tonight, I throw myself on the cedar for the good of the village, so that Ewig will continue to bestow his blessing upon you all, and you can live in peace and harmony for another five annuls."

"Seems to me that if the villagers just hadn't tried to kill Ewig, we'd all be better off right now."

"Thorna!" Sister Milka said. "Quiet your tongue."

She held up her hands and walked out the door again. "If I can't talk, then I guess we're done here."

"We are not!" Sister Milka shouted. "We must bless the cedar!"

"Why?" Thorna said at the doorway. "There's no blessing in marching to your death. Calm your own conscience, but mine is clear."

If she were any other in the class, save Bella, she would have been beaten mercilessly for her outburst, but given her position, all Sister Milka could do was watch her stomp down the stairs and walk down the dirt street, out of sight.

# Chapter 7

It was impossible to blame the children in the school for being part of the system that would kill me in a matter of hours. They believed authority, and authority told them my death was a good thing, that they should dance in the streets and celebrate.

Even then, as I walked past them out of the schoolhouse, I could tell they felt something was wrong. As they said their final prayers to me, several of them broke down and cried, and the voices of others warbled, but, aside from Thorna, none of them protested.

Why would they? Their parents didn't protest, or even voice concern. They couldn't even look me in the eyes as Sister Milka and I walked across the square to the City Hall that sat equidistant between the church and the school.

"They really are going to send you off in style," Sister Milka said. The other adults had the courtesy not to smile, except for Sister Milka, who let her satisfaction be known. She beamed with pride at her accomplishment.

"Yes, it's quite a nice-looking celebration of my death," I replied, immediately regretting my words. I had never said anything like it before, but talking to Thorna, and my mother's confession, created a bitterness that bubbled in my throat.

"What a horrible way to think about it." Sister Milka looked sternly at me, and then shuffled forward to a cotton candy stand. "One please."

The young man behind the counter swirled a pink cloud and handed it to her. When she tried to pay, he pushed it away. "My treat, sister."

Sister Milka turned and handed it to me. "They aren't celebrating your death, my dear. They are celebrating your life, and the gift you are giving them."

"I thought I was too fat for my dress already?"

"What's one more sweet treat at this point? You clearly need it to counteract the bitter pill you've swallowed this morning."

I picked a piece of cotton candy off the top and popped it in my mouth. It was overly sweet. So much so that it nearly turned sour in my mouth. I did not like the taste, but I choked it down, much like the false words that came out of the sister's mouth.

"I know they aren't celebrating my death," I said, trying to backtrack out of a fight that wasn't worth fighting. "And I appreciate their offerings."

It was untrue, but I had heard this speech too many times before, about how the villagers cherished me and my gift, and that I would never be far from their thoughts. I even believed it, until the memory of Freja faded from the town's memory, and I realized the adults barely remembered the names of the girls who were sacrificed in their youth.

"That's my girl." She patted me on the head softly. "Such a good child."

It was better, in the end, to placate her ego instead of being forced to listen to her insipid words spoken with little passion, especially today. After our tea at city hall, I would be free for a few hours to say my final goodbyes to those close to me, until I had to meet back at my house for one last bath, and to put on the last clothes I would ever wear.

City Hall was wider than the church, but plain, and stout. Every office of the government could be found under its roof, but we were only interested in a single office today: that of the mayor. Our feet echoed against the marble floors, which our founder had brought in special from the capitol. We followed the hallway past several heavy cedar doors, polished until they shined, until we reached one twice as wide as the others, with the word 'mayor' etched above its simple frame.

"Your best behavior," Sister Milka said. "Do not embarrass me."

Gods forbid. This was her victory lap as much as my farewell tour. She needed to be seen by everyone of import in town, so they could laud her ability to mold me from wet clay into perfect cedar.

Sister Milka opened the door to the Mayor's office, and walked to the reception desk at the front of the room. When Tilda saw us, she waved and stood.

"You're here!" she squealed. "The mayor is so excited to sit down with you. He's been talking about it all morning. Let me go get him."

She disappeared behind another heavy door, and Sister Milka turned to me.

"You never answered me."

"Excuse me?" I asked.

"You need to be on your best behavior. No sassing back like you did outside. Do you understand?"

"Yes, ma'am," I said without hesitation. One moment of breaking was too much for her. She expected perfection at all times. Even today, my emotions didn't matter. There was no room for slippage.

It was how she controlled me, and I let her. I wished I was as strong-willed as Thorna, but she had broken me like a stubborn pony.

No, that's not true. I was never that strong. I always needed Sister Milka's approval, even as a child. I yearned for it.

That was how she brought me under her thumb, and she kept it there by using my mother, and even Leyhan, as bait. In that way, Thorna was right. The way to avoid her control was not to love anyone. That was impossible for me. Even after all my mother did, I still loved her. Even after all Sister Milka did, I loved her still. I hated myself for it, but that was the truth.

The heavy door to the mayor's office swung open and a big, jolly man with a glistening red face and thick mustache sashayed out of the room. He wore his broad shoulders well, and a wide grin that told me he didn't care even a little bit about the fact I would die soon.

"Morning, Gilda." He shook my hand with both of his, completely enveloping them in his meaty paws. His callused palm scratched mine, but I simply smiled. "We have quite a feast planned for you, my girl. We're going to send you off in style." He turned to Sister Milka, mercifully letting me go. "And you, Sister Milka. You get lovelier every time I see you."

"You're too kind, Mayor."

"Please, come inside." He spun around and led us into his office, which was nearly as large as my house, with a desk in the center of it, and a table near the door with tea set out for the three of us, along with three places for the city elders, who hadn't made their presence known yet.

"My." The mayor eyed me up and down. "I believe this is the most beautiful of all the girls you've ever brought before me."

It was a compliment, and I tipped my head to acknowledge it, but what did it matter if I was pretty? An ugly girl could die as easily as a beautiful one. Did it make it sadder that I was pretty? If so, that was pathetic.

"Are the elders joining us?" Sister Milka asked excitedly. "I haven't seen them since the last ceding."

"I set them places, but they are very busy, you know, keeping the city running." The mayor picked up his tea and turned the conversation. "We've had a lovely boar brought in from the Bronkian region, they really do make the best meat there, and our best cooks have been preparing a collection of meats, cheeses, and wines the likes of which we've never seen before, at least not in this city."

"I appreciate it," I said, before taking a sip of tea. He had prepared black tea, with no milk or sugar, and it was bitter on my tongue. "You don't have to do all this for me."

"Nonsense!" the mayor shouted. "Every feast must be better than the one before it. That is the way." He cocked a crooked eye to me. "Are you not excited for it?"

"Excited?" I said. "To die?"

The mayor nearly choked on his tea. Sister Milka shot me a devilish look, but there was nothing she could do to me now. My death was certain already.

"Well, no, not that." He stammered as he tried to collect himself. "For this feast, of course. It's quite a big honor. Not many people have a whole day devoted to them."

"Most people won't be eaten by a dragon tonight, either."

"Gilda!" Sister Milka shouted. "This is inappropriate." She turned to the mayor. "I'm so sorry, Mayor. I'm not sure what's gotten hold of her. It must be all the excitement."

"Quite alright," the mayor said, settling down. "This is a big night. Lots of nerves for everyone."

"Yes, that must be it. Not that I will be eaten alive in a few hours." I took a sip of the tea. "This is lovely. Thank you, Mayor. I have never had its equal."

It was a little rebellion. Nothing like what I imagined Thorna would say, but for me, it was like setting the whole of the room on fire, and for the first time all day, I felt slightly better.

# Chapter 8

"I don't know what that was about," Sister Milka said when we finally got back outside after tea. The mayor had cut our meeting abruptly short after we sat in silence for a good five minutes after my outburst. He claimed he had emergency business he needed to attend for the feast, but I knew the truth. I made him uncomfortable. Good. I shouldn't be the only one. "But you rightly embarrassed me."

"I'm sorry, sister," I replied. "Perhaps the excitement of tonight has taken control of me. I didn't sleep well last evening. I shall be sure to take a nap before we reconvene for the festivities tonight."

This seemed to appease her. "Very well. I suppose it's not the worst thing in the world. I shall meet you back at your house for the final dressing. Enjoy your time off."

"Thank you, sister."

"And remember. Loose lips sink ships."

Every day of my life had been scripted since before I could remember. The nuns told me what to eat, what to wear, even what to think. Today, they gave me two hours to say my goodbyes to everyone and everything I had ever known. To make peace with my death. It was the most free time I had since I could walk, and I decided to spend it with my best friend, Leyhan.

Most people kept me at arm's length. It was much easier to send a stranger to their death than a friend. However, even in a town that kept me at arm's length, Leyhan still found a way to burrow his way into my heart.

Cedars weren't supposed to fall in love. My heart was meant for the great dragon Ewig, and yet, over the years, I fell madly in love with him. I have often thought about telling him, but it would only break my heart, and his. If he didn't feel the same way, then I could never look him in the eyes again, and if he did, then we would have to live with the fact that I would one day become a sacrifice to the great dragon. We would never have a love story that ended in anything but tragedy.

"This is awful," he said, as he swung his feet over a short cliff that looked down at a creek on the edge of town. It was the furthest I had ever been from home. Every time I thought about venturing further, the foreboding sounds of the forest gnawed at my stomach and ate my resolve.

"I know it does," I replied.

"We could do it, you know. We could just go, and never look back."

"Then Ewig would allow the volcano to burn this city to the ground, or he would do it himself."

"So what?" he replied. "You hate all these people."

I shook my head. "I can't have that on my conscience."

"You would rather die than feel guilty?"

I sighed and looked down at the peaceful water that flowed under me. The babbling brook snaked through our town and washed itself out into the sea a hundred miles away.

"Better on their conscience than mine."

"They have no conscience. I thought you would have learned that by now. They have brainwashed you, Gilda."

"Maybe," I replied. "But this is all I know. You're very sweet for wanting to burn it all down for me, though."

"Screw being sweet," Leyhan said. "I'm trying to save your life."

I placed my hand over his and felt a shock of electricity shoot through me, so powerful it took my breath away.

"I don't have much time left, Leyhan. I would like to enjoy what little I have in peace."

"Peace is good." He nodded, before a wicked smile crept across his face. "You know, if you weren't a virgin, then you couldn't be sacrificed."

I couldn't help but laugh. "Yes, you have made that case before."

He shrugged. "I'm just saying. It's a thing, and we should consider it. I'm willing to make that sacrifice for you."

"Yes, I know. And then we would both be executed, along with everyone we love."

"I wouldn't let that happen."

"You can't stop it. Nobody can. This is the way of things. It has lasted for a hundred years, and it will last for a hundred more."

"No." He shook his head vehemently. "I don't believe that. Even if you won't go with me, I won't rest until this whole system is burned to the ground."

"That's a nice thought. I hope you and Thorna can make it happen."

Without another word, he grabbed my hands in his and pulled me close to him. Tears welled in his eyes as he stared into mine. I thought he would say something, but every time he opened his lips, nothing came out.

"I love you," he finally uttered, stammering over his words. "I have loved you since the first time I saw you when we could barely stand, and I will love you for the rest of my life. I couldn't let you die and not know that."

It was everything I always wanted to hear, and yet there was no happiness at his confession, just a cutting pain that pierced my gut. I wanted nothing more than to confess my love back to him, to wrap him in my arms and ravage him on that cliffside, but none of that would change the facts. We couldn't run. I hadn't worked a day in my life and didn't have the stamina to escape the town for long, and he was a baker, who didn't know the first thing about forest living. Even if we could make it to the next town, there was no guarantee they would take us in, or protect us.

If they did, we would spend the rest of our lives looking over our shoulders, uneasy in the knowledge that we caused the deaths of everyone we knew. If we didn't, we would have to keep running until we found a safe haven that might never come. No, it was not meant to be.

"You know I only love one, dear sweet boy. I am bound for Ewig. He is my betrothed."

His hands shook as he took them back. "I...don't...understand how that could be. He's going to devour you. I could give you a life."

I placed my hand on his shoulder. "You will love again."

He shook his head violently. "Not like this."

"Better than this, I promise you."

"And what is that?" His words were biting. "The promise of a woman who chooses death over me?"

The church bell rang in the distance. Four bells, which meant it was time for me to leave and meet Sister Milka.

"It's time." I pushed myself up off the ground and brushed the muck off my dress. "Save a dance for me tonight."

"I will save every dance for you, for the rest of my life."

"I don't need you to do that." I smiled at him. "Maybe just for the rest of mine."

# Chapter 9

I looked beautiful. Magical even. I hated to say it, but the tailor knew what he was doing, and when I was introduced to Ewig, I would take his breath away, I was sure of it. Then, he would take mine away.

"You truly are a vision," Mom said as she peeked on from the door.

"Isn't she, though?" Sister Milka replied with a smile. "I am prouder of her than any I have ever tutored. I dare say she would buy us a decade, if such a thing were possible."

That wasn't the compliment she thought it was, but I nodded graciously all the same. "You are too kind, sister."

"Would you mind terribly," Mom asked, "if I talked to my daughter for a moment before you take her to the ceremony?"

Sister Milka furrowed her brow and looked toward the cuckoo clock in the corner of the room. "I suppose I can allow it, even though Gilda was late returning from her sojourn this afternoon. Come, Seamus. Away. Let them have their space."

"Thank you again," I said, swirling the hem of my dress as I moved from side to side. "It truly is a marvel."

Seamus nodded and tipped his cap to me before making his way out of the room. When the room was clear, and the front door latched with a thud, Mom closed the door behind me.

"I don't think we should end it like that. I don't expect you to forgive me, but I need to know you don't hate me."

I looked at myself one more time in the mirror. Even now, hours before my death, people made asks of me. Even at the end I couldn't keep anything for myself. I wanted so desperately to yell at her, to scream and rail, but when my eyes connected with her doughy face, I didn't have the energy to despise her.

"I want to hate you, but what good would it do? The damage is done. I can't run. I can't hide. I can't allow somebody else to die in my place. I can't stomach the idea of the entire village burning under Ewig's flames because of my selfishness. Had I left with dad all those years ago, before they filled my head with pleasant lies and dutiful truths, maybe I stood a chance, but now, there is nothing I can do. I am locked into my fate." I sighed. "I have made my peace with that."

"I don't know if I have," mom said.

"That is your burden to bear. Don't put that on me. For my part, I forgive you."

She held up her hands. "I'm not. I just— wonder what might have been."

"That is the prerogative of those who get to live through the night." I stepped off the stool and opened the door. "Now, if you will excuse me, I would like to be alone with my thoughts before the end. It is the last chance I will have to be alone for the rest of my life, and I feel like I've earned it."

"Okay," Mom said sadly, walking toward the door. "I love you."

"I know you do. I love you too, even though you are sending me to my death."

"I—" she started, but I slammed the door in her face. I couldn't listen to her say another word without unleashing on her, and that wasn't the last image I wanted my mother to have of me, nor mine of her.

I listened for her steps to soften as she walked down the hall. When she was out of earshot, I sat down on the edge of my bed, and cried, careful not to drip my tears on my lovely, delicate dress. It really was beautiful. It was a shame that in a few hours it would be stained red with blood and torn into a thousand pieces.

# Chapter 10

They threw a good party in honor of my death, I had to give them that. I was too small to appreciate the last feast, but now, I hated to admit I was impressed with the quality of everything. They had hired a ten-piece chamber orchestra from the capitol to play for the night, and a roasted pig hung from a spit in the middle of the celebration.

There were moments, in the thrall of dancing and eating, where I even forgot this was my last night on Earth, but then somebody would come back and solemnly shake my hand, or I would catch Thorna's eyes as they tracked mine disapprovingly, and it would all come crashing down on me. That was when I would have another glass of blueberry wine, or stuff another piece of sweet bread in my mouth and feel better for a moment.

I had been to enough weddings that I knew the bride and groom had to walk the floor and make small talk with the guests, and this was no different. Though my betrothed was nowhere to be seen, I had to spend time with each of the attendees, shepherded by Sister Milka, who was careful to move me along before I had a chance to dour the mood of the revelers.

It was a whirlwind before I finally sat down on the dais, after the sky had darkened to night and the stars came out to say their goodbyes after the sun took its final bow to me. The raucous rabble had died down, replaced with a solemn din from the tables scattered around the square. I sat on a long table, my mother on one side, and Sister Milka on the other. The mayor sat next to my mother, and the three town elders, two women and a wrinkled man, all so old it looked like a stiff wind would break them apart, rounded out the table. They only seemed to make it out every five years, and the years had not been kind to them since our last meeting.

"This food is the best, is it not, Gilda?" the mayor asked.

"Oh yes," I replied. "You were not wrong. You truly spared no expense."

"You are worth it," Mom said before I could reply.

"Yes," I added. "I'm worth everything, except saving."

At that, the mayor gave a tight nod and stood. This was not polite dinner conversation. He crossed the dais to a podium set up against the far edge and cleared his throat.

"Honored citizens." His voice boomed. "Thank you for coming and celebrating our most sacred festival. This is a solemn occasion, but also a joyous one, as we accept the sacrifice of one for the life of all. So, please, let us raise a glass to the guest of honor, Gilda." He turned to me. "Your family's noble sacrifice will never be equaled, and for that, we are forever in your debt."

The collective raised their classes, and the din of glass replaced the low hum of chatter. A chorus of "here heres" came from the group, followed by the swallowing of wine.

"Now, I would like to welcome Elderman Florence to give a final blessing before we conclude the celebration and begin the ceremony."

A chair slid on the far end of the table, slowly creaking as it scraped against the wood of the stage. A woman's voice groaned as she stood, and her legs knocked together as she rose to her feet. Even expending that much effort was a struggle and looking at her made me reconsider whether it was truly a curse to die young, if it meant not growing to become a prisoner of a decrepit body.

Elderman Florence shuffled slowly across the stage. Her once dark brown hair was now a mess of grey and white, which matched her gaunt, sickly skin, full of deep wrinkles across every inch of her. If she was beautiful once, those days were long gone, and all that remained was a hunched husk of a woman, whose every breath was filled with pain. The thought of her life being filled with agony soothed me. I wanted nothing more than those responsible for my death to suffer, and that she found no respite from her pain made me feel slightly better about my plight.

Finally, after a long silence as the townspeople watched their matriarch teeter as she took slow steps toward the podium, Elderman Florence gripped the side of the stage and opened her mouth to speak. After a long, pained sigh eked out of her mouth, she took a breath.

"I have watched 16 children sacrificed to the great dragon Ewig. If I were born two months earlier, then I would have gone to my death instead of my friend Petunia. It is never easy, and every ceding is filled with solemn reflection as much as the rapturous joy that we have earned five more years of freedom, prosperity, and abundance." With great struggle, she turned to me. "Gilda, my child, your sacrifice is a gift, a blessing, and a curse. Few have ever worn the weight of your life on their shoulders, and few will be remembered in our collective consciousness like you will be for your gift to us. Tonight, you ascend into the sky to take your place among the great heroes of our age." She turned back to the group. "I have lived long, and know the greatest gift is sacrifice. We all must sacrifice. I sacrificed my peace to maintain the oral record of our people, while you sacrifice a long life to save us. We three elders, along with the whole of our village, accept your sacrifice, and our ancestors will welcome you with open arms."

How did they know that? How did they know I would ascend into the Heavens? How did they know our ancestors would be waiting for me? They didn't. It was all just platitude, something to make them feel better about killing a child.

"And now," Elderman Florence said, "I welcome you to go back to your homes, and light your shrines to the cedars, and to your ancestors, letting them know to accept a new angel tonight."

With that, the band played a final song, a slow, plodding number that felt like a funeral dirge. It was the same song that carried the other cedars to their deaths, and when it started, my stomach fell to my knees.

Sister Milka grabbed my hand and lifted me to stand. I caught eyes with Leyhan as she turned me to the back of the stage and regretted not leaving with him. I regretted it all. Every minute of my miserable life. I wanted to scream, but when I opened my mouth, nothing came out. My voice had been stolen from me, as sure as my life would be. I struggled against Sister Milka's weight as I reached the bottom of the stairs, but I was met with four soldiers, dressed in the glittering gold of the capitol, and I knew there was no hope for me left, not that there was any to begin with; I was always destined to die. I just hoped my death really did mean something.

# Chapter 11

The walk of shame. That's what Thorna called it five years ago when we were watching Renata take her last steps up to the tip of the mountain. Officially, it was called the procession of the cedar, and right now, around Thestral, 11 other girls were headed to their deaths, the great sacrifices to the dragon lords who showed their mettle against the gods themselves.

It was supposed to be a march of pride, but Thorna was right. I felt more shame than anything as the guards surrounding me stopped at the edge of town, in front of the archway that marked the beginning of the rocky road that led up to Ewig's keep. The squad of golden clad soldiers broke apart to reveal Sister Milka standing behind them. Next to her, my mother, Leyhan, Thorna, and Bella stood in a jagged line, holding torches. They were my bearers, chosen to carry the burden of my confessions, and bring my light to the community. They would witness my ascension, until I disappeared into the cave, and sit until the following morning to make sure I didn't exit again.

Across from them, the mayor and elders stood. They would leave when I started up the mountain, but it was tradition for them to see the cedar off and wish them good fortune in the great beyond. Behind them stood four younger officials, who would take their mantle as witnesses until morning to keep my chosen bearers honest.

"Are you ready?" Sister Milka asked, as was the tradition.

"I am ready, sister," I replied, though it was a lie.

Her down turned lips rose into a smile, and she took my hand. She guided me toward Elderman Florence, who grabbed my hand with both of hers. The folds of her skin rubbed against my smooth palm as she shook.

"Petunia was my best friend when I was your age." She sighed. "Our birthdays were a couple months apart, and I think every day about how, if our places were switched, she would have been here, and I would have died in that cave so many years ago. I don't know which is more agonizing, the pain I live with, missing her, or the pain she suffered at the great dragon's hand."

"It was hers," I replied, without question. "Her suffering was worse, and unnecessary."

She patted my hand. "Yes, it is easy for one as young as you to say such things, but she lived a short, brilliant life, and I still wake up, some seventy years later, in a cold sweat, her pained screams ringing in my ears."

I smiled my sweetest smile and leaned in so that only she could hear. "Good. I am glad she haunts your memory."

I pulled away from her and moved down the line. The other two elders gave little but a curt shake and nod, accented by the sobs of Elderman Florence, who started to cry when I broke from her. This wasn't odd as she always cried at these things, at least as far back as I remembered, and now I knew why.

"May your journey be swift, my dear," the mayor said, shaking my hand with vigor as he smiled brightly at me. "Tonight, you will look down at us from the stars and know you saved us all."

"That's not the comfort you think it is, but thank you, Mayor."

Sister Milka slid me out of his grasp and pulled me away from him. Behind his crazed eyes, I knew he had more to say. People didn't talk to the mayor that way, and he was none too pleased, but he was sending me to my death, so he would have his revenge.

Sister Milka spun me around and the tears welled in my eyes almost immediately as I watched my only friends staring back at me. I wanted to stay strong for them, but my body had other ideas.

I knelt to Bella. I couldn't believe that in ten years' time she would be in the same position as me, and that a decade ago I was standing where she was, barely understanding what was happening.

Bella raised her hand to show me a white daisy. "I picked this for you."

I smiled and slid the flower into my hair, behind my left ear. "I'll treasure it always. When you look into the sky tomorrow, look for the girl with the flower in her hair, and that will be me, looking down on you."

She leapt forward and wrapped her arms around me. "I don't want you to go."

I hugged her tightly. "I know, baby. It's okay, okay? It will be okay."

I unlatched her from me as her sobs rose into a wail. I turned to Thorna, who fell to the ground to comfort Bella. "This isn't right."

"No," I replied. "But it is my choice."

She sneered at me. "It's funny you think that. Any lie to make it feel like you weren't tricked into this, though, I guess."

I dropped my head. "Please, I don't want to fight."

"I know," she replied. "But you going to your death quietly perpetuates the idea that we should suffer our fate, too, and I hate you for that."

"I'm sorry," was all I could think to say. I didn't know why I was apologizing for dying, and yet, it seemed to placate her slightly, though she didn't connect with my eyes again, instead choosing to comfort Bella.

That was her choice, and as one of the only people in the world who could understand what was going through my mind, I had to let her express her feelings however she chose, even though I knew she would regret it when I was gone.

"I'll miss you."

"No, you won't," Thorna said. "That's the whole point. You'll be dead. You won't miss anything. We'll miss you, though, until it is our time to die."

Sister Milka helped me to my feet as Leyhan rushed forward and kissed me full on the lips. Everyone gasped around me, and while I was surprised, I couldn't help letting out a soft moan as I melted into him. This was my first kiss, and it would be my last.

I barely heard the gilded guard gliding around me, my head lost in the ecstasy of his lips against me, and Leyhan struggled against them as they pulled us apart.

"We had sex!" he screamed. "She can't die tonight, because she is not a virgin!"

"No!" I shouted. "It's not true!" It was an instant death sentence to defile a sacrifice. "He's lying to protect me!" I turned to Sister Milka. "Please, you have to believe me, I would never—"

"Quiet!" Sister Milka shouted, turning to Leyhan. "When did this happen?"

"This afternoon, by the creek. We confessed our love for each other, and she gave herself to me. We gave ourselves to each other."

Sister Milka's scowl turned into a laugh, as she cackled into the Heavens. "Oh, my child, do you not think we would be watching at this late hour to make sure she stayed chaste?"

Dread fell onto Leyhan's face. "But—no, it happened!"

Sister Milka walked forward and caressed Leyhan's. "Poor, misguided boy. Do you think you're the first to fall in love with one of my girls?" She snapped her fingers. "Let him go."

"Wait?" I said. "You aren't going to hurt him, are you?"

She turned to me. "Of course not, dear. Your purity saved him. Now, before we have another commotion, I think it's time for us to leave. The moon is high in the sky, and your betrothed is waiting." She motioned to my mother. "Say goodbye to your daughter, Odine."

My mother stepped forward as the soldiers blocked me from the others. She grabbed me around my neck and pulled me close. Hot tears fell from her face to my cheek.

Mom squeezed my hands. "I wish I had let you go with your father."

I wanted to tell her that I wish so too, or that she should have thought of that sooner, but it was too late for that. "I love you, Mom."

After a few seconds, Sister Milka's bony fingers tapped my shoulder, and I turned to her. I took one last look at my bearers. Thorna had extended herself to wrap Leyhan into her arms as well. She looked at me with a fiery stare that spoke volumes. Why are you the only one not trying to save yourself was what it said, clearly and plainly.

Perhaps they would find a way to save each other, because there would be no salvation for me.

# Chapter 12

The stone was cold against my feet, and slippery on the sheer ballet flats they gave me for the journey. I would have thought that the path would be smooth and easy to navigate, but the terrain was harsh and unforgiving. On either side of the rocky path, the cliff face dropped precipitously into the abyss below. Thin wooden handrails were all that prevented me from plummeting into the sky below.

"How is it that nobody has fallen in all the years you've done this?" I asked, voice shaky.

"The will of the dragon lords," Sister Milka replied from behind me. "They desire this to be done, and so it shall be done."

That was the kind of country fried bologna that masked as clarity for religious zealots like Sister Milka. Either that or it was the type of lie they shoveled into the mouths of young girls destined for death to strengthen their resolve before the end.

"We used to have a bridge, with easily designated handrails. However, we found that it was then too easy to reach the cave of the great dragon. Children would scamper up to Ewig's cave on dares, and lovers who run away to have secret trysts. You know how the young are, impetuous and foolhardy, willing to tempt fate, so we destroyed it some time ago."

I didn't know what she meant. I never had the chance to be impetuous or foolhardy. I had the weight of my whole village on my shoulders since the moment I was born. I wasn't like Thorna, who could rail against her responsibility, or Leyhan, who evaded his because he was a boy, able to throw rocks from the safe distance of manhood, where harsh words were never quite so acerbic as when they came from a woman.

I took a step forward and my slippers slid on a wet rock, splaying my legs, and dropping me to the ground. A sharp pain shot up my butt and through my back as I yelped out in pain.

"Silly, foolish girl," Sister Milka said, every ounce of compassion drained from her voice as she lifted me up. "The last thing that Ewig wants is a bruised bride."

I spun on my heels as I yanked myself free. "Stop calling me that. I'm not his betrothed. I'm not his bride. I'm his supper, and the least you can do is stop lying to me as I walk to my death."

"I do it for your benefit. Sweet lies are more comforting than bitter truths."

"Then don't say anything," I grumbled, carefully stepping over the rock that nearly caused my demise. "I would prefer brutal silence to your lies."

Which would be worse? Falling down the side of a mountain, crashing into every rock on the way down, or being eaten by a dragon? At least with the dragon, he might take pity and snap my neck quickly. With the rocks, you were completely at the whim of nature, and it was a cruel, unkind mistress.

Sister Milka stayed quiet as we made our way up the final ascent to the cave, muttering prayers to herself I couldn't intuit. The last few meters were steep, but there were plenty of rocks to aid in my climb.

Ewig's cave was smaller than I imagined, barely taller than me, but deep enough that it was consumed with darkness. There were no torches on the sides of the cave to lighten my path.

"This is where I leave you," Sister Milka said. "Is there any message you would like me to carry back to those you love?"

I thought for a moment, then shook my head. "I have said everything I needed to say to them."

"Then..." She raised her arms into the air. "Oh, great dragon lord, we offer this girl to you, to be your eternal bride, until you release her. See that she is cared for, and loved, for all the days of her life, and with her willing betrothal to your greatness, look over our town for the next half decade hence. Bring us bounty and good fortune as we offer one of our cherished daughters as a sign of our fealty to you." She touched my forehead. "In the name of the old gods and the new, amen."

She looked at me one last time, cupping her rough, pruny hands on either side of my alabaster face, before falling silent, and I knew it was time.

I turned from her without a word, and walked into the darkness, toward my destiny.

# Chapter 13

*Every five years, the Dragon Lord Ewig must be appeased with a sacrifice to renew his pact with his chosen people. I have been chosen to fulfill a great purpose, to act as kindling on the pyre of our love for him.*

Every morning since I was a child, I would say those words to Sister Milka as she eyed me carefully, looking for any sign of faltering, as she did with every part of my life. I would say them again before every meal, and before I laid my head down for the night.

Before I could speak, she would say the words to me as she cradled me in her arms, and when I was still older, toddling around the room, she would have one of the older cedars say it to me as she watched them.

I didn't understand what the words meant at first. I didn't know what it meant to be a sacrifice, or that I would die when I was fifteen years old. It wasn't until I watched Freja walk up the side of the mountain with Sister Milka when I was five, and saw the nun return without her, that it started to sink in what would happen to me in ten short years.

It still felt like a lifetime away. Time moved slowly when I was a child. Every day felt like an eternity, and I thought I had all the time in the world. It wasn't until Renata went to her death that the years began to speed up for me, little by little, until the last year felt like it went by in a second.

As I stepped through the dark, dank cavern, where I couldn't see two feet in front of me, my life began to flash in front of my eyes. I saw myself as a baby, and at my first solstice. I saw my first day of school, and my last. I watched myself move through the world, among the people, but not one of them, and all I could think the whole time was how frighteningly little of my life there was, and how I wasted so much of it.

The scenes continued through my memory, and I took note of how the townspeople, those same citizens I was about to save, looked at me with cold, calculated indifference that bordered on cruelty. When I reached for them, they jumped from me, as if I were a leper with a contagion that could be passed on to them.

Why was I so intent on saving them when they clearly felt so little for me? Why, even now, do I feel an insatiable desire to die for these people, who cheated me out of my life so callously?

I didn't have to keep going. I could simply sit in the cave until Sister Milka left, and then I could slip out and escape when nobody was looking. Maybe I would die in the woods, or maybe I would die on my way down the mountain, but I wouldn't have to die in such a horrible manner as being ground up by the gnashing teeth of a dragon.

As I stopped to ponder betraying the village, a loud grumble came from further into the cave, and I jumped at the sound of it. A scream eked out of me and bounced off the cave walls, announcing my presence. All my thoughts of abandoning my fate and running away vanished with me. This was what I had been born to do, this was my destiny.

Perhaps I should feel happy at the thought of fulfilling my purpose. Few ever got a chance to fulfill their destiny, especially at such a young age. My mother didn't seem any happier for living so long, and Elderman Florence seemed positively aghast at the length of her life.

I placed a shaky foot on the ground as I stepped closer to the sound of the dragon. Another growl rocked the dark cave, and a light flickered in the middle distance. It was warm in the sticky, damp cave, and though I knew that it came from the dragon, my body craved it after walking in the cold, night air.

My next step forward was easier than the last, and the one that followed it even easier still, until I glided with ease toward the fire set in the darkness. The heat from the fire washed over me and illuminated the cave. In the light, the cavern glowed and shimmered with white, red, green, and blue. I slid my hand over them to find rubies, emeralds, diamonds, and sapphires embedded deep in the walls, enough to rival the wealth of a small nation, and yet, they laid undisturbed.

"Oh my," a deep voice growled, loud enough to startle me back to attention. "Is it time already?"

I turned to find a great clearing, and in the middle, curled up around a fire, was the great green dragon, leathery black wings wrapped around him as his yellow eyes glistened in the fire. He seemed to smile at me with ragged, jagged teeth inside a jaw bigger than I was tall.

"Great gravy," I exclaimed, almost immediately covering my mouth. "I'm sorry, your grace. That was—I didn't mean to be impolite."

He sighed loudly and pushed himself to stand. Large, black talons extended from his scaly paws, razor-sharp and able to fell me with a single swipe.

"Well, I'm about to kill you, so let us not stand on ceremony."

He was so callous about my death. It unnerved me, but I swallowed my fear and opened my mouth to recite the verses. "Great dragon Ewig, I offer myself to you, for the protection of my people, as payment for your grace, and your love. For your fealty, I offer my blood, as a symbol of the bond between your chosen people and your grace. As it washes down your throat, remember your oath to them. I offer my flesh, as remembrance of the protection your countenance provides from the looming volcano threat that has long plagued us. As it coats your tongue, allow our pact to be renewed for another half a decade, and know that all we do is in service to your glory. I offer my soul to you, complete and unmolested. As it touches every inch of you, know that we are powerless in your company, and look to you to light the way for us."

"That was horrible," he said. "There was no passion behind your words, and I nearly fell asleep by the end."

"I'm sor—"

"Death." He cocked his head to one side. "Is that really what you wish, cedar? For me to kill you, I mean?"

"Ummm..." I replied. "I don't understand the question."

"Are you daft?" he asked, his voice booming louder. "Have they sent me an idiot this time around? How sad."

"No," I replied defiantly. I would be killed, but I would not be insulted. "I am not daft, nor am I a dullard."

"Am I speaking a foreign tongue then?" he growled. "I know so many tongues that I sometimes slip into the wrong one."

"Again, no. I understand you clearly."

"Then answer the question. Is it truly your wish for me to kill you so that those that sent you to your death can prosper?" He slid his long neck down so that his enormous face hovered inches from the ground, his hot breath crashing into my face. "Could you really be so full of grace as to willingly give your life for them?"

"N-n-n—yes."

"You seem hesitant."

"Nobody has ever asked me that question before," I replied, closing my eyes. "I am sorry. I wasn't prepared to have a conversation with you. I thought you would just eat me."

"Nobody has ever asked if you wanted to die?" He cocked his head quizzically. "They simply expected you to go to your death with grace without asking what you wanted?"

I dropped my head. "It is tradition."

"Ah yes." His head rose again. "And tradition is everything, isn't it?"

"Yes, my lord." I curtsied to him, my heart racing in my head. "I am ready to die."

"Then let us get on with it."

# Chapter 14

*No, no, no, no, no. This wasn't what I wanted. Run, already. Feet! Run!*

But my feet wouldn't move. Fear stuck them in place.

As I watched the great dragon Ewig rise up into the air and unhinge his jaw to swallow me, all I could think was how much I wanted to run and hide, but my body was frozen in terror, trembling at the sight of the incredible beast in front of me. Was this how the others went, peeing themselves with fear, regretting every moment of their lives, wishing they weren't cowards enough to suffer their fate?

"Oh, quit playing with the child, Ewig," a woman's voice grumbled from across the cave.

The dragon looked down at the figure standing in the cave entrance behind him and rolled his eyes. His jaw rehinged and he slunk back down.

"You're no fun," he growled at her. "I get so little time for theatrics. Couldn't you just let me have my moment?"

"No," the woman said. "I thought we agreed not to scare the child."

"You agreed to that, I never did. I get so few chances to be worshipped, Renata. Why must you take that from me?"

"Because it's awful and gross."

"Wait," I said, stepping forward. "Renata?"

The figure stepped into the light, and though she was older, and her hair was wilder than I remembered, it was surely Renata, the last girl to be sacrificed to the great dragon lord.

"Hi, kiddo," she said, popping her hip as she walked to me. "I've been waiting for you."

"Am...I dead?"

*Yes, that had to be it.* I blacked out as the dragon ate me, and I was now in the afterlife, being met by my friend who would lead me into the great beyond.

Renata looked at me for a second, then laughed. "Oh god, you were right, Ewig. They really are so funny when they come here for the first time. Was I really this naïve?"

"Moreso, if anything," Ewig growled as he curled back up. "Now take her away before I change my mind and eat you both."

"Whatever." Renata rolled her eyes before she held out her hand toward me. "Come on, Gilda. Let's get you settled."

I grabbed her hand on instinct and she pulled me past the fire and the great dragon curled up around it. He lost interest in me and nuzzled into the crook of his leathery wing. From the side, he didn't look very intimidating, and as he snuggled against a rock, he looked more like a cat than a ferocious fire lord.

"Uh...what is happening?" I asked as my brain caught up with my feet moving in concert with Renata's. "I watched you go to your death. I watched the fear in your eyes. I waited for a whole night to make sure you didn't escape."

"It's nice to see you, too," Renata replied.

"I'm sorry, it's just...you should be dead."

"She's right," Ewig said, groggily as we passed him toward the cave entrance behind him. "I should have killed you all those years ago. I would have been rid of a big pain in my ass."

"Please," Renata replied. "You love me, and you know it."

"Barely worth it," Ewig replied.

"But it was worth it," she countered as we disappeared into the cave behind Ewig.

This cave was dark, and I wondered how Renata was walking so smoothly and confidently in the dim cavern.

"Are you sure this isn't the astral plane?" I asked, confused.

Renata laughed again. It was the kind of carefree laugh of somebody who was truly free. I had never seen her so uninhibited and light. When I knew her, she was as tight-lipped and reserved as I was.

"Oh god no. Nothing like that." She stepped over a large rock and turned to help me navigate it. "Did you eat today?"

"Yes," I started, but then I thought better of it. "I had breakfast, and some cotton candy.

Then I drank blueberry wine and some finger foods at the feast, but I wouldn't say I'm full or anything."

"I didn't eat much at my feast." She bopped herself on the head with her palm. "Every time I sat down to get take a bite, I was pulled in one way or another by somebody who wanted to ask some stupid question or shake the hand of the latest cedar. Then, when we finally sat down, I was too nauseous and scared to eat anything."

"That is very relatable." I looked back at the cave. "Is that why he didn't eat me? Am I not plump enough? Are you going to fatten me up so he can feast on me later?"

She turned and placed her hands on my cheeks. "Breathe. I know this is hard to believe, but you're safe now."

"Safe?" I asked, confused. "What does that even mean?"

I haven't felt safe my whole life. I felt cared for, sure, but there was always a dagger hanging over my head, and there was a purpose I was being groomed for, to die at the right time.

"It means nobody is going to try and kill you anymore." She pulled me forward. "Now come on, I have to introduce you to the girls."

"Girls?"

She didn't answer me, but I began to hear voices as we moved further through the cave. The voices grew with the light, until the cave broke into another clearing, except in this one there were a half dozen women sitting behind a long table filled with food.

"Welcome home."

# Chapter 15

*What was happening?* I stood over the cliff behind Ewig's lair that led down to the dinner table below, where four women sat, passing out meat and veggies to each other, like they hadn't just risen from the dead, and like their existence was the most normal thing in the world.

"Are these...cedars?" I asked, tears filling my eyes at the mere thought of all the girls we had sent to their death over the generations being alive and well.

"They are," Renata said with pride. "Would you like to meet them?"

I nodded. "I would."

My heart was filled with joy as she led me across a rope bridge and down a set of wooden stairs to the table where the four other women sat. When they saw me, they turned and smiled, waving pleasantly and welcoming me to their feast.

"This is Mari," Renata said to a blonde who didn't look much older than she was. "You never met her. She was the sacrifice right before Freja, right before you were born."

Mari held out her hand delicately and I shook it. Her smile was coy, and demure, in a way I only wished I could pull off. I always felt like a lumbering brute playing at being graceful.

The woman next to Mari had wild, curly, gray hair and dark green eyes. She wore thick clothes, like Mari, but hers were covered in mud and dirt, while Mari's were pristine.

"This is Fadia," Renata said. "She was a sacrifice a—"

"Long time ago," Fadia interrupted while ripping off a bite of meat from a rabbit leg. She didn't seem to mind the juice dripping down the sides of her mouth and made no motion to wipe it off. She held out her hand and the grease dripped off it as well. After I shook it, Mari handed me a napkin to wipe off my hand. "Nice to meet you, girly. Man, they sure did a number on your complexion. Did you ever get an ounce of sun?"

"Be nice," Renata said. "It's not her fault she's pasty."

"Enough with her," a dark-skinned woman shouted. "Get over here, new girl. Let me get a look at you."

"That's Selma," Renata said, bringing me over to her. "She's the healer around here. She takes care of all our bruises and ailments, among other things."

Selma latched onto my neck and pulled me close to her. She cocked her head one way and then the other, running her eyes over my face. "They kept you healthy, that's for sure." She pulled my hands to her face. "Never did a spec of work, did you?"

"No," I replied. "It wasn't allowed."

The girls all chuckled. "Well, that'll change now, dearie."

Renata slapped Selma's hands away from my neck. "Don't scare the poor girl. Ewig already did a fine job of that." She pulled me away. "Fadia was a sacrifice forty-five years ago, and it's been thirty for Selma."

"Wow, and they've lived here for all this time?"

"Give or take."

"Can somebody pass the vinegar?" an older woman with braided hair asked as she held a bowl of salad. "The lettuce is a bit bitter tonight. I'll make a note of it."

"And that's Nur," Renata said, picking up a glass bottle full of vinegar and handing it to her. "Here you go."

"Thanks, hun," she replied. "You look like you can appreciate a good meal."

"Umm..." *Was she calling me fat?* "Thank you?"

"The new stray looks hearty." Fadia shouted. "I like that. How do you feel about farming, girl?"

"Umm, I'm fine with it, I guess." I replied.

"Don't mind her. She is always trying to get people to tend her garden with her."

"You have a garden?" I asked.

"We have all sorts of surprises up here," Selma said as she grabbed a loaf of bread. "I made all these bowls and glass using the heat from the volcano under us."

"That's impressive," I said. "Your mom would be proud."

Selma tucked her blonde hair behind her ear. "Don't lie to me. They didn't care about me much. They preferred when I was silent and obedient."

I shook my head. "That's not how I remember them. They talked about you all the time."

"And what do you know about my family?" Fadia said from the other end of the table before Selma could reply.

"You had one sister, and a brother. Your mother and father worked as sheep herders before you were born."

"And what did they do with the fortune I died to give them?" Fadia asked, bitterness on her face.

"Squandered it," Renata said. "That was true five years ago, and it's still true now, I'm sure, right Gilda?"

I nodded. "Unfortunately. They still have the house, and the town still makes payments to them, but, well, they aren't the most respected people in town."

"No, they wouldn't be," Fadia said. "I hoped maybe the last five years allowed them to turn their life around."

"And what of the town?" Mari said. "Tell us any gossip you can remember. It is so droll and boring up here I could almost die."

I recounted as much as I could about the last five years. I told them about Thorna and Bella, and all the other people in town. My heart was filled with great happiness at the thought I would see them both again soon enough.

"And what of Freja?" I asked. "Where is she?"

The cave went silent, as their eyes ping-ponged back and forth. Finally, Renata spoke. "A couple of years ago, some of the girls chose the path of the forest."

"What does that mean?" I asked, sliding into a seat next to Renata. "What is the path of the forest?"

"It is a choice we all have to make, including you," Nur said. "You have lived under a tyrannical rule for a long time, and now it's time to give you a choice."

Selma stood and walked toward the cave entrance behind her. She picked up a large backpack, made of leather. "No doubt you have seen that this cave is made of precious gems that would give any of us enough wealth to live like a king. Inside this pack are enough clothes and gems to make it to the next kingdom and set you up in a life of luxury."

"Or you can stay here," Renata said. "And live with us, the only people in the world who know your plight, and what you have been through.

It's not a glamorous life, but we maintain okay. We cook, we clean, and we even hunt."

"You hunt?" I said, excitedly.

She nodded, pointing to the meat in the middle of the table. "I caught all that myself. We each have a job to do here, and because of that, we get along."

"That sounds hard. Why didn't you all leave with the others?"

"Where am I going to go?" Selma asked. "This is my home."

Renata grabbed my hands. "Somebody needs to stay here and take care of the new people, like you. Otherwise, what would happen to you?"

"I would survive," I said.

Mari walked over to Selma and grabbed the bag. "If you believe that, then you can go, like others before you have. We are not here to force you to do anything."

"But if you stay," Fadia said. "Then there are rules."

"Rules?" I asked.

"To keep us all safe," Renata said. "If the townspeople knew they were being tricked, then they would be rightly pissed."

"That's rule one," Mari said. "You have to remain hidden. You can't reveal yourself to anyone—"

"—Not your best friend," Renata cut in. "Not your mother. Not even that nice boy who seemed to have eyes for you. What was his name? I always liked him."

"Leyhan," I replied. "I really cannot see him again?"

"Absolutely not," Fadia said. "Even if you leave, you can't see him. Otherwise, you will endanger us all. Understand?"

"Yes," I said.

"Seriously," Renata said. "I will walk you to the edge of the forest and make sure you don't come back. If you do, I'll kill you myself."

"H-h-has anyone ever come back?"

Nur shook her head. "No. They stayed gone. The last thing anyone wants is to see the people who just sent them to their deaths."

"But not everyone is bad. Leyhan tried to save me," I said.

"No buts," Mari replied. "You can't see him, any of them, no matter what."

"You are dead to them," Fadia said. "It's how it must be for our protection, and theirs."

"Okay," I replied, dropping my eyes. "I guess I can live with that."

"Just remember," Nur said, "you are living with it, which is more than the townspeople wanted for you."

"It's really not all that bad. I promise." Renata gave me a small, sweet smile. "You barely remember them after a while."

"Did you really forget your family?"

"For the most part. It's a process." Renata cleared her throat. "Rule two, no disturbing Ewig unless he calls for you or you're feeding him. He tends to burninate people when he's grumpy."

"And he's always grumpy," Mari said.

"That's the truth," Selma added.

"That makes sense," I replied. "I don't really want to see him, anyway. He's kind of scary."

"Good," Nur said. "Let's keep it that way."

"Final rule!" Fadia exclaimed. "We all pull our weight. No slouching."

"Honestly," Mari said, rubbing her hands, "that's the hardest one. I used to have such beautiful hands."

"So, I'll have to work?" I asked.

"That's right," Renata said. "You'll assist each of us at first to see what you're good at, and then you'll be able to do your own thing. You haven't worked a day in your life, but that's about to change." She stopped. "You're going to hate it, and then you'll grow to accept it." She smiled. "Eventually, you'll take pride in it. Then, you'll love it."

"But if I leave..." I said, trailing off.

Selma walked forward with the pack in her hands. "If you leave, you'll be able to lead a life of lavishness and luxury. Those pretty hands will stay as perfect as they are now."

"Why did you stay?" I asked Selma.

"I don't much like people," she replied. "But I like my sisters here, and I never minded hard work. I always found being rich frightfully annoying. I hated brushing my hair a hundred times a day and sitting in silly rooms doing silly things. Here, I get to do something meaningful, but it's not for everyone, obviously."

The other girls nodded in camaraderie with Selma, as if they all had their own reasons that more or less matched hers.

"It's completely your choice," Renata said, grabbing my hands tightly. "But I hope you'll stay. I have so much to show you."

I smiled. "I've never had a choice in anything before. Every minute of my life has been planned for me since I was little. It's a little terrifying."

"I remember that feeling. It's scary and liberating at the same time, right?"

"Yes, that's exactly it," I said with a smile. I looked around the room at the powerful women all around me. In their own ways, they grew from the naïve girl who was to be sacrificed to the great dragon into strong women, and I never knew I always wanted that so badly for myself.

"I think I'll stay."

"Wonderful," Renata said. "Then, let's finish dinner, and I'll show you to your bed."

# Chapter 16

I didn't eat much at dinner, even though my stomach growled hungrily for me to feed it. I didn't want to seem ungrateful to my new coven, and so I made sure to pick and shuffle my food around the plate, so that it looked like I ate more than I did.

"Newbie cleans," Fadia said as she walked out of the back of the cave, followed by the others. Selma left the backpack on the edge of the cave "just in case I changed my mind".

Eventually, it was just Renata and I standing in front of the table, piled high with discarded carcasses and the remains of food.

"Aren't you going with them?" I asked as I picked up the food from the table.

"Don't be silly. Until tonight I had to clean every meal, and before you can take over for me, I have to show you how to do it right."

She walked over to the edge of the cavern and knelt in front of a metal wash basin. She grabbed one of the rope handles and instructed me to get the other. We brought the basin against the wall closest to Ewig's lair. A stream of hot steam shot from one of the holes in the rock, and we placed the basin atop it.

"It'll take a minute before it gets hot enough to clean. Then, once we're done, we bring the water to the garden and leave it for Fadia." She pointed to the bones on one of the plates. "Just make sure to keep the bones away from the ruffage, which we'll use for compost."

I picked up one of the rabbit bones. "What do we do with these?"

It was a question I never thought to ask back at home. My mother or somebody in the community would take care of it. I didn't have to sully my hands with such things.

"We'll grind some of it to make glue and other things, but most of it will get buried in a pit. I'll show you where you can bury it without attracting predators or townsfolk."

I looked over at her as we waited for the water to boil. "Have you all really been living here for a hundred years?"

"Yeah, basically."

"That is unfathomable to me," I replied. "How did it all start?"

Renata held her hand over the water. It wasn't quite ready, so she sat back down next to me. "You've no doubt read the books. I think we even read them together."

I smiled at the memory. "We did. It was nice."

"I don't think I have nice memories." She shook her head. "Every good memory I have was tainted with the knowledge that everyone in that town wanted to kill me."

"I didn't."

"No, you didn't. That's why you and the girls are the only people I can stand being around." She stood up and walked back over to the basin. She nodded briskly and beckoned me over. "Scrape everything off into two piles. One for veggies and another for bones and skin. We don't have much time before it gets scalding."

I spent my time scraping all the plates onto the ground, while Renata washed them in the basin. She placed the finished ones on a clean rock next to the steam and showed me where to find rags to dry the dishes. We were halfway done when I remembered she didn't answer my question.

"Far as I can gather, Ewig's never once eaten a cedar. I don't know if the same can be said for his brothers and sisters, but I can only assume they're not quite as forgiving." She furrowed her brow. "Can you believe they wanted to watch us die in the beginning?"

"The townspeople?"

"That's what Ewig told me." She nodded. "At the first ceding they wanted to watch the sacrifice; that it was their right, but he told them no. He took the girl back to his cave and...well, the rest is history."

"I can't believe I'm saying this, but if that's true, then Ewig is kind of a hero."

Renata burst out laughing. "Don't let him hear you say that, ever. If there's one thing he hates, it's hero worship—well, no. He hates many things. That's one of many things he hates."

"So, everything we know is a lie then," I said, placing another dry plate on the ledge to cool.

"Not everything. You know the town would kill you, and that's all that really matters, in the end. You know who will stick up for you. You said somebody didn't want you to die? Did he stick up for you at the end?"

"Yes." I smiled. "Leyhan. He said we slept together to save me."

Renata could barely contain her laughter. "Oh god, and I'm guessing Sister Milka loved that."

"Oh yeah. Her face went beet red for a moment, but in the end she didn't believe him. Said she had people following me, and knew he was lying." I took a breath. In the frenzy, I never stopped to think about what would happen to him. "Leyhan will be okay, won't he?"

She nodded. "He's not the first one to lie to save somebody he loved. He'll get a few lashes in the town square and told never to think of you again. The hardest part is the knowledge that he'll do it, too. He'll forget you ever existed."

"I could never forget him."

"Give it time." She stopped. "Do...any of them talk about me?"

I opened my mouth to give pleasing lies to her, but that wasn't the kind of woman Renata was, and I didn't want to start off lying to her. "You know the town. They don't want to think about anyone."

"And my parents?"

I bit my lip. "They had another kid, when you were gone. Long enough from the ceding that she couldn't be a sacrifice. I don't think they ever got over you, but Abigail is adorable."

"I hope she has every luxury I never enjoyed."

We finished cleaning and scraped the compost into one bucket, and the bones into another.

"Nobody tried to save me, Gilda." Renata's face contorted into a scowl, and then softened. "At least you had one person who did. You can keep that in your heart for as long as you can, until it naturally fades with time." She picked up the bucket and headed for the cave entrance that led out onto the side of the volcano.

"Not bad for a first day, right?" Renata said as she grabbed a torch from the cave entrance and turned down a path. "Ready for bed?"

I nodded. "So ready."

"Well, you can't sleep yet. We've got a couple chores left, and then I'll show you to your room."

# Chapter 17

The bucket of bones was heavy against my left hand, and I dragged the wash basin in my right, helping Renata move the remains of dinner down the sloped ridge outside the cave a little at a time as my strength would allow. My hands were burning by the time Renata stopped at an alcove cut into the volcano.

"Are we there yet?" I puffed, heaving my chest, exhausted.

"You've been asking that for the last fifteen minutes, but yes, we're finally here." Renata walked into the alcove and her torch lit up a garden, filled with lettuce, tomatoes, and corn, among other crops. It was much larger than I thought possible on the edge of a volcano. "I know you're tired, but chores are good. You'll be exhausted at the end of them, and you'll sleep like the dead."

She turned with a smile, but her words didn't sit well with me. I was supposed to be dead, so sleeping like the dead wasn't something I was interested in at the moment. I wanted to sleep like the living.

"Sorry," she said, seeing the upset oozing from every pore. "Slip of the tongue."

"No, it's okay." I sighed. "This is all just new to me. I thought I would be dead right now after being ripped apart by a dragon, and to have a reprieve, to meet all of you. It's a lot."

"I know." She walked toward the far end of the garden and popped open the top to a bin, like the ones I had seen around town, but never bothered to learn about. "It will get better, easier, in time."

"I hope so." I stepped forward. "What are you doing?"

"Compost," she said. "This stuff will all decompose, and then we use it for fertilizer."

When she finished with the garden, we continued down the path. Mercifully, she left the wash basin and compost in the garden so my hands could get some relief. I looked down at them in the firelight when we finally stopped again. Broken calluses made my hands red and raw. Even touching them, or squeezing my palms together, made me wince in pain something fierce. I had never done a day of manual labor before, and even an hour of it made every joint in my body ache.

Renata walked into the next alcove and picked up a shovel. She spent a few minutes digging deep into the ground, and then burying the bones inside of it.

"Help me cover it up," she said, pointing to the pile of dirt. "Just kick it in. It's very cathartic."

I didn't believe her, but I couldn't argue with her, either. She was the only lifeline I had to my other life, and I couldn't lose her. Freja was gone with the other cedars, and even Mari was sacrificed before I was born. Renata was the only one I knew, and thus the only one I trusted, so I needed to stay close to her, and that meant doing as she said, no matter what. I was always good at that. Sister Milka often praised my ability to follow directions.

Renata leaned against the shovel as she watched me rear back my leg and shove a little dirt into the hole with my leg. "Like this?"

"No." She shook her head. "Really kick it, like a soccer ball."

"I've never kicked a soccer ball."

"Well, you've seen other people do it, right?" She asked. "They really smash it with all their power."

"Won't that send the dirt flying everywhere?"

"Absolutely!" she said, nodding. "It wouldn't be cathartic if it wasn't messy."

I didn't know how kicking dirt everywhere would help fill the hole, but I did as I was told. I spun my leg backward, swung it forward with all my might...and missed it completely. So completely that I slipped on the ground and fell on my butt.

"Ow," I said, as Renata rushed over to me. "That was not very cathartic."

She bent down and helped me up. "Maybe you need to work up to that."

I brushed the dirt off myself. "Maybe."

She finished filling the hole and then we started trekking back up the hill, where I had seen the others go when they left dinner. When we got to the cavern, Renata walked inside and snuffed out all the lights, except for the one she had in her hand.

"We usually eat before nightfall, so we don't bring attention with the light, but tonight was special. This whole week is special as we bring you into the fold."

As she made her way around the cave, I turned to look out across the mountain and the forest below. In the distance, a lake separated us from the next country over, giving our village a natural protective barrier between any invaders to the east, and the mountains on either side of us gave a natural ridge that insulated us from the south and north as well.

I had never seen the lake before, or the dense forest in front of it. We were forbidden from crossing the mountain ridge to the other side for any reason. This was Ewig's forest, and even the sentinels and soldiers of the village didn't dare encroach on his space for fear of his retribution.

"It's beautiful, isn't it?" Renata said as the soft light of her torch found my face.

I turned to her. "It's beautiful. Absolutely and truly breathtaking."

"What do you think so far?" she asked. "Of all this?"

"Well, compared to death, it's pretty great."

Renata laughed. "I can't argue there. Chores are just a little bit better than death, but tomorrow, I'll show you how to fish, and that will be better."

"How do you do this?" I asked. "All of it. From where I'm standing, it seems impossible."

"Do you want me to answer that, or do you want to go to sleep?"

"Oh, definitely sleep," I replied without missing a beat.

She nodded and led me up the path a little way. My legs burned and ached when we finally got to the next cave entrance. I had never walked this much in a month, let alone a single day.

Inside the cave lay twenty or so beds. The other girls speckled the room on a few of them, but many were empty...too many of them, it seemed, but I bit my tongue as it felt like a question I shouldn't ask about, at least not yet. Renata led me to a bed, where a nightgown, towel, and brush were laid out on top of the sheets.

"This one is yours," she said, then turned to a sloppily made bed across from it. "This one is mine. Goodnight, Gilda. Today was a big day, but tomorrow, you start a whole new life."

# Chapter 18

Renata was right. The minute my head hit the soft, down pillow, I was out like a light. Luckily, I had changed into an old nightgown Renata provided for me and brushed my teeth before I fell into bed. Otherwise, I would have woken up in the same dirty dress I had worn the night before.

I don't remember falling asleep, and I don't remember dreaming, but when I woke the sun pierced through the cave and hit my eye. I stretched until my legs and arms were off the small bed, and the sleeves on my nightgown rose to my elbows.

In my old life, my bed was so big that I couldn't reach the end of it on my biggest stretch, but this new bed was significantly smaller, cramped even, and while I could lay flat out on my old one, I ended up having to sleep cramped in, with my knees nearly in my armpits to fit.

I pushed my arms up and stretched my back with a big yawn. When I was done, I craned my neck around to see that nobody else was still in the cave. Their beds had been made with varying degrees of smoothness from Renata's ratty mess to Nur's perfect fold tucked in tightly.

There was a small, bubbly stream coming out of the wall in the back of the cave where I brushed my teeth and washed my face. The water was warm, but not scalding, so it was perfect for jolting me awake against the cold whipping through the cave. Though there were multiple blankets afforded me, I still woke with a chill that rippled through my whole body. *Would spring never come?*

When I was properly awake, I walked outside to see the sun cresting over the horizon, kissing everything it touched with orange and red beams of light. The lake shimmered like diamonds in the distance and the trees underneath the volcano swayed in the morning breeze.

"Yup," I said as I took a big, long stretch. "This is definitely better than being dead."

"Oh, good. You're up." I turned to see Renata bringing a pot of piping hot coffee up the hill to me. The steam from it rose high into the air, and the two tin cups she carried in her other hand clanged against each other as she walked. Draped over her elbow hung a change of clothes. Nothing fancy, just a pair of brown trousers and a green wool shirt, but they would bring some much-needed warmth. "I brought you some coffee and a change of clothes. Mari has been up since before dawn finalizing the measurements. If they don't fit, let me know."

They fit perfectly fine, and when I was done changing, I met Renata back at the entrance at the cave, where she poured me a cup of coffee.

"I have never worn pants before," I said, pulling at the crotch a little.

"How do they feel?"

"Scratchy." I lunged forward after taking a sip of coffee. "Constricting, but warm."

"Mari makes all the clothes herself, and she darns anything that needs mending too, so make sure not to say anything like that in front of her."

"I would never," I said, taking a sip of coffee. "I have always wanted to try coffee."

"And?" Renata asked.

"It's quite bitter, isn't it?" I asked.

"Only the way Nur makes it," Renata said. "I would kill for some milk and sugar, but we have to make do without it up here."

"I'll bet they have it in the city," I said, turning back to the mountain.

"They sure do," she said. "Freja is probably awash with the stuff right now."

She looked longingly into the middle distance, not at anything in particular, just letting her eyes unfocus as she stared off into space. After a moment, she blinked and sighed deeply, before a softness came back to her face that went missing for a moment.

"Are you ready to fish?" she asked.

"Absolutely," I replied, though I wasn't quite sure. I had never been into the woods before, even at home.

"Then come on. Mari needs your shoe size so she can cobble some shoes for you. In the meantime, you can wear some of my old ones. They are worn and torn past repair, but better than walking in those terrible ballet flats along the forest floor."

Renata reached under her bed and pulled out a pair of tattered boots, made of dark brown hide, and we started down the mountain. When we reached the main cave, Nur was inside, working over a black cauldron while Mari sat at the table with a pile of clothes and shoe leather.

"About time you got up," Mari said. "How are the clothes?"

"They're fine," I replied, trying hard to say only nice things as they rubbed coarsely against my back and arms. "Very warm."

"They look like they are riding up on the crotch. I guessed you were about the size of Ingrid, but your torso must be longer. I'll find another pair and take them out for you. Meanwhile, sit."

She kicked a chair over to me and I sat down. She brought over some rope and wrapped it around my foot, taking measurements on a piece of parchment that had almost no room left to write on it. Every inch seemed to be covered, but she found small places to make notes across the cluttered page.

When she was done, she shook her head. "I knew those slippers were too small for you. They pinched, didn't they?"

"A little, maybe?" I said, more asking that stating.

"Is Mr. Dunnerton still the cobbler—" She saw my eyes drop from her gaze. "What?"

"That's my dad. He left soon—he wanted to get me out, and they found out. My mom—" I tried hard not to cry. "Mrs. Ventrel is the cobbler now."

"I see," she said. "My parents never tried to help me escape. They were too wrapped up in their own wealth, poisoned and blinded by it. You should feel lucky your dad tried to do anything."

"I don't feel very lucky," I said.

"You're here now," she replied. "And I'm the best tailor in the whole region. Best cobbler too, and I work exclusively for the six of us."

"Is she done?" Renata asked. "We have to get out on the lake."

"Not before she eats," Nur said, sliding a bowl of porridge under me. "It's not much, but it's hearty." She turned to Renata. "Don't throw the bones away tonight. I'll need them to make some new stock."

"Got it," Renata said. "Hurry up, Gilda, shovel your food. It's an hour walk to the bottom of the mountain, and another to the lake."

I nodded and shoveled the stew in my mouth. It wasn't as hearty as the type I was used to, but it was flavorful enough, and I said my thanks to Nur when I was done. Then, I threw on Renata's old boots. They were small in the front, and too large on the sides, but they would work in a pinch.

"I'm ready," I said, standing when I had laced the shoes.

"No, you're not," Renata replied. "But I love the attitude."

# Chapter 19

On our way down the mountain, we waved at Fadia tending to her garden, and picked up the empty bucket we used for bones. I thought Renata was exaggerating when she said it took an hour to get down the mountain, and though I couldn't tell exactly how long it took, it was a long time, and Renata was less chatty than last night, lost in some thought or another as we clomped forward.

Maybe it was because I started whining after about fifteen minutes, as the sun stopped being pretty and started being hot and muggy. She was quick to point out last night that I hadn't worked a hard day in my life, and my body wasn't used to it. Back at the village, whenever it got hot and muggy, I was confined to home, and the elders sent somebody over to fan my body to prevent overheating. Now, I was stuck with Renata, who had no such sympathy.

"You're going to learn quickly that this world is a harsh place. Now that you aren't being fattened up to die, nobody cares about you except for how useful you are, and right now you're about as useful as a penis on your elbow."

When we reached the bottom of the volcano, I fell onto a cool rock as Renata retrieved two fishing poles and water skins from inside a hollowed-out tree. She handed one of the skins to me, and I sucked it down greedily.

"If this is how you act on the way down," Renata asked. "Then how are you going to do on the way back up?"

It dawned on me then that we would have to climb back up the mountain when we were done, and that meant hard slog miles up, and I could barely handle what little we walked last night.

"I think you'll have to leave me here to die."

She took another sip of water. "Don't think I wouldn't if I didn't fear you would run back to the village."

"I would never do that!" I shouted.

"Shhh," Renata replied. "You can't squawk like that out here."

My eyes narrowed at her. "What happened to the kind woman I met last night?"

"She's still in there," she replied. "But I'm all business right now. If we don't fish, we have nothing but veggies to eat tonight, and that is no sort of life I want to lead." She held out her hand and lifted me up. "Besides, I have to beat the little princess out of you."

I had never been into the forest by the village before, instead confined to the village and outlying farms. I had heard stories of the fantastical creatures that lived inside of it, and how Ewig protected us from them since I was a child.

The sounds of trees rustling, and strange sounds, rankled the hairs on my neck as I stepped forward with Renata, but watching her confidently strut forward gave me the bravery to do the same, and with every step I took, my head rose higher.

"Luckily, the church has convinced the villagers that the volcano, and everything past it, is Ewig's territory, so even the bravest of them don't come here. We're alone."

"Then why can't I...what's the word you used...squawk?"

"There's a lot more than villagers to be scared of in these woods. Bobcats, bears, and all manner of predators roam these woods that would make your head spin if you saw them. Even if we don't need to protect ourselves from other humans, nature is dangerous."

"That's what they used to tell us. I thought it was another lie."

A twig snapped under Renata's foot. "Not everything they said was a lie. Much of it was just a perverted version of the truth. They wanted you timid and scared so you wouldn't flee. What they didn't tell you was the real danger lurked inside the city walls."

"They protected me, at least."

"And they worked to kill you. They smiled at you, and fed you pretty lies, but their intent was always villainous. At least out here, things are as they seem."

By the time we reached the lake, the sun was high overhead. Renata cursed herself in waiting so long to leave and cursed me for making her delay past sunrise. She grumbled and complained, but when she got to work, she was a good teacher.

She reached into her pocket and pulled out a handful of metal hooks, untangling a couple and handing me one before bending her fishing line to the ground and sitting cross-legged next to it. "Watch me."

I joined her on the ground and watched her tie a complicated knot in the fishing line. I tried to replicate it, but when it was done, Renata just shook her head and made me do it again. Each time I failed, she undid her own line and replicated it for me to watch, moving slower and slower until I finally noticed the subtlety of her pattern and was able to replicate it.

"Good!" she said. "Finally, but it took me longer to learn my first time. Now, try it again, until you master it, while I go find some worms."

She stood up and disappeared into the woods as I kept untying and retying my line until she returned a while later. At the bottom of the empty bucket, she had placed a pile of dirt. Upon closer inspection, the earth moved and wriggled, undulating to reveal a dozen pink worms. My instinct was to shudder and turn away, as I had at home, but Renata pulled my head back with her dirt-caked hand to look at the bucket.

"I know it's kind of gross," she said. "But you need the stomach to look at them for the next part, which is much grosser."

Renata let my head go and dug her dirt, pulling out a wriggling worm from the bucket and holding it up for me to see. I nearly threw up at the sight of it, but then did wretch when she took the worm and pressed it firmly on the hook until the metal pierced through it.

"Now, it's your turn."

I shook my head. "No way. I can't do it."

"That's a shame. Because we're not going back until you catch a fish, and we can't catch a fish until you hook a worm onto your line."

"Can't you do it for me?"

She nodded. "Yes, very easily, but I won't. Give me your hand."

I fought against her, but she was much stronger than me, and when she yanked me forward, my body complied. She placed my shaky hand into the bucket and pressed it to the dirt. The worms writhed and slithered over my hand, and I gagged again, pulling my hands away, desperate to find relief from the disgusting feeling. I couldn't beat Renata, who used her weight to push my hand down even further until, eventually, the writhing no longer forced me to wretch.

"Better?" Renata said when she saw my calm face.

"A little."

"Good, now pick one up."

My fingers shook as they gripped around the worm, and I pulled it out. After the rain, these worms littered the streets around my house, and they always disgusted me when I would find them wriggling around the streets. Now, I held one in my hand.

"Okay," Renata said calmly as I held the worm. "Now, grab the hook."

I didn't think I could do that part with how much my hand shook, but she guided my hand until the hook hovered next to the wriggling worm. In my whole life I hadn't killed a single thing. I made my mother kill spiders and flies, even ants caused me to scramble up a couch. Now, in my new life, I was about to stab a worm through the stomach.

As Renata moved my hands together, they began to shake violently and uncontrollably, but I didn't drop them from her clutches. I let Renata push my fingers to the hook and apply enough pressure that the hook slid into the worm's body. I thought it would jerk, or scream, but it didn't seem affected by the hook at all.

"Very nice, Gilda." Renata's voice was even calmer. "I passed out the first time I tried it, and the other girls wouldn't even try it."

"Was that even an option?" I asked. "Could I have not done this?"

"Of course," Renata said with a smile. "But aren't you happy you did?"

"Absolutely not."

"I think you're lying," Renata said. "Not to me, but to yourself. Wasn't it a little exhilarating to do something you never thought you could do?"

I looked back over the woods, and then down to the worm. I had never been through the woods. I had never been a mile from my house before. This was the furthest I had ever been from anything I ever knew, and when my stomach settled, I realized my pulse was racing, and there was a mad giddiness in my heart.

"Maybe," I replied finally. Not able to give her the satisfaction.

"Stopping lying to yourself is a good first step. Now, all you have to do is catch a fish and we can go home."

# Chapter 20

As Renata taught me how to cast my line, I learned two things. The first was that fishing was all in the wrist, and the second being that I had no coordination, and even less wrist strength.

"It's like snapping a whip," Renata tried to tell me.

"I've never done that either!" I shouted. "Why would I have reason to snap a whip?"

"I guess that's a good point."

She showed me how she snapped her wrist at least a dozen times, and even guided my hands, but even with her help, it took me forever to get the flick right. When I finally flicked my wrist and cast the line the right way, watching it sail through the air, I jumped up and down with glee and pride, nearly dropping my fishing line in the process.

"Don't get too cocky," Renata told me. "You haven't caught anything yet."

Renata was a machine, catching big, floppy fish consistently throughout the day. Every time she reeled in a new catch, she forced me to pull it off the line and throw it in the bucket. The first time I reached under the fish's gill and pulled out the hook, my stomach lurched forward, and my heart broke watching it flop around, gasping for air until it died, but after the fifth time, my heart had hardened enough that it didn't bother me nearly as much.

Once the sun fell behind the volcano at our backs, Renata had filled up the bucket, and I was still struggling to catch even a single fish. She no longer even held her rod once she cast. Instead, she laid against a rock as the sun drifted away.

"If you don't catch one soon, we'll have to walk back in the night, and the last thing you want is a bunch of nocturnal predators chasing after you with a bucket of chum causing a stink."

"I'm tryin—" I started, but then I felt a yank on my line. My eyes went as wide as Renata's as she leapt up and scrambled over to me. "Something's tugging on the line. What do I do?"

"Pull it in, duh!" she shouted. "Reel it in."

I slammed my hand on the reel and started to wind it back up as the line pulled and yanked around me. Renata grabbed me around the waist to stabilize me and pulled me backward away from the shore as the line popped up from the ground and flung into the air, waving back and forth as I reeled it in harder.

When the reel was finally in, we both had a big laugh at the tiny fish on the end of it.

"That's got to be the smallest fish I've ever seen," she said as she pulled it off the hook. "But a deal's a deal, and that is a fish. Let's head back."

She tossed the tiny fish into the bucket and picked it up. Together, we began back through the forest. We didn't talk for a long while, but I was proud of myself, and I let that pride carry me through the trees, and past the sounds that even this morning would have caused my knees to quiver.

"I'm proud of you," Renata said. "None of the other girls would even try it. What do you think about hunting?"

I nodded. "I'll try it. Can we do it tomorrow?"

She shook her head. "Not yet. The other girls have laid claim to you first, but this weekend I can show you how to set a snare and use a bow. You probably won't get the hang of shooting arrows so easily as fishing, but at least you can lay a trap and catch small game."

As we walked, I heard rustling in the bushes. I turned to watch the bush on my left move and jut as it shimmied.

"Get down," she said, moving me away from the bush. A few seconds later a small rabbit hopped out, looked at us, and hopped away. "Phew."

"It's nice to see even you get scared," I said with a smirk.

"I'm not scared," she said, defensive. "You better not tell anyone either. Remember, I know how to use a bow."

By the time we reached the cave, the sun had set. Fadia was no longer at her garden, and was instead seated at the table, around Nur and the others, who were enjoying a bowl of soup and some salad.

"We didn't think you'd ever get back," Nur said. "We started without you."

"Glad you weren't worried," Renata said. "I brought fish. We'll gut them and eat a few tonight. I'll leave a few for Ewig, the rest to get smoked for the winter."

"Gut?" I said, cocking my head to one side.

"Oh yeah," Fadia said. "You're going to hate it."

Fadia was right. I absolutely hated gutting fish. Renata brought me to the far end of the kitchen and handed me a serrated paring knife. Then, she showed me how to pull the backbone out of the fish and clean its organs out so that only the tasty bits remained. I had never thought about where my food came from, or how terrible it was to look a dead thing in the eyes and be responsible for mangling it.

"Are you sure you're okay?" Renata said, watching me go white. "I can do this part if you want."

I shook my head, trying hard to keep the bile from rushing into my throat. "No, I did the catching. I'll do the gutting, too."

After the deed was done, we brought what was left over the fire and cooked it over a spit.

"Don't let it sit on any side too long," Nur said. "You don't want it to dry out. Ewig hates that."

"We all hate it," Selma said. "Not just him."

I hadn't noticed it before, but in the din of the room, I heard Ewig snoring coming from the end of the hallway.

"Does he really just lay around all day?" I asked.

"Most days," Fadia said. "Sometimes he goes away and brings us back gifts, like those nice beds, but usually he just lazes around."

Renata stood up and slid the fish off the spit. She placed them on a big tray and slid them onto the table. Then, she took three of the biggest fish, still raw, and placed them on a metal serving tray.

"Go bring this to Ewig," she said, handing it to me.

"M-m-me? Are you sure that's a good idea?"

"Why not," Nur said. "He's gotta eat, and somebody's gotta feed him. You don't want to see him hungry. He's a big enough sour puss in the best of moods."

"I don't know—" I started, before Renata shoved the plate into my chest.

"Nur is right, somebody has to do it, and today it's you. You can't be scared of him, and the sooner you get over that irrational fear, the better. Otherwise, you'll end up like Mari, who can barely look at him."

"I can so!" Mari stammered. "I just don't wanna is all."

"See?" Nur said, jokingly. "Irrational."

Irrational? He was a huge dragon with razor sharp claws and teeth. My fear of him was absolutely rational, and so was Mari's. However, I didn't want Renata to see me break. She had already seen it too much today. Maybe that was her plan, to see how far I could go before I snapped.

I wasn't going to snap. I wasn't some brittle thing. Not anymore. Now, I had burned my old life, and my new one had risen from the ashes. In this life, I was fearless.

"Fine," I said, turning from them. "I'll do it."

# Chapter 21

My hands shook and knees trembled as I made my way through the cave back toward the lair where the great dragon lord Ewig lived. He hadn't killed me, and that meant he must not have been completely evil, and yet my stomach fell to my feet as I marched toward him just like when I entered the volcano for the first time.

There was a cool breeze in the cave opening where the girls ate dinner that counteracted the sweltering heat in the rest of the cave. The further I got from them, the more sweat beaded on my arms and dripped from my forehead.

Still, even with the heat of the volcano, Ewig still had a fire raging, and when I stepped into the clearing where he laid, curled up around it, the warmth from the fire washed over me, choking me and causing me to gasp for relief.

When I finally caught my breath, I looked up to see Ewig's glowing yellow eyes staring at me, the glint of the fire reflecting from them on one edge, and my frail body in the other.

"Hrm, they sent you tonight, did they?" Ewig asked.

I nodded, stepping forward carefully. The tip of my toes met the front of Renata's boots, causing me to wince as I stepped, but I tried to cover it with a placid smile.

"Yes, sir. I brought you some food."

"Please don't call me that." His voice echoed through the cave, deep and low. There was hardly any emotion on it. "Leave the sirs for the knights and nobles."

"Yes, si— I'm sorry. It's just, I was told I have to address you since I was a child, and to do so with reverence."

"Reverence?" His hot, hollow breath smelt of a warm hearth after a cold, winter day. "They speak with reverence, and yet they won't do the one thing I asked and leave me alone. Instead, they insist on sending silly, little girls here who expect me to eat them." His eyes narrowed at me. "Do you know how insulting that is?"

I shook my head. "No. I thought that was what you asked for, si—Ewig."

"I asked them to leave me alone, but the proclamation from my stupid sister said one girl every five years needed to be sacrificed, and they were too scared of retaliation to let it go. And now, I have a gaggle of you to look after. Maybe I should have just killed you all and gotten my peace. It's what the rest of my family would have done."

My eyes dropped with my head. "I appreciate that you didn't kill me. I know you could have. I know you still could."

His voice groaned a discontented sound. "We all have the capacity for killing. With the right motivation, you could kill me."

I gasped, shaking my head furiously. "No, my lord. I never would do such a thing."

He looked me up and down with just a slight move of his eyes. "No, I don't suppose you would. In the same way, I would not kill you. I gave up that life long ago. Now, what have you brought me?"

I stepped forward and placed the fish down in front of him, before backing off slowly. I could barely hold the plate still long enough to lay it without it clanging on the floor.

"You still fear me," he said as I slipped back toward the wall. "That is probably for the best. I have done things that would make your blood curdle."

"I...I have heard of your greatness."

He grabbed one of the fish with his teeth, carefully, and flung it in the air, before catching it in his mouth and swallowing it whole.

"The things I have done are not great. I am not proud of them. They haunt my mind and turn even the most pleasant dream into a nightmare." He looked up from his meal at me. "When you are as old as me, you regret much. I almost pity that now you will grow old enough to feel the pangs of regret as I do."

"Please don't pity me for that," I said. "I am thankful you have not eaten me."

He swallowed another fish. "Even though it means a life of manual labor, with girls who fear and detest me?"

"They don't—they can leave any time they want and live a good life—they stay because they care about you, and each other."

"That is a nice thought, but you have not been here long. I will wait until you have stuck around for some years before I take your opinion seriously. No offense, but your naivety is sickening."

I slid my foot in the sand below me. "I'm sorry. I wasn't trying to sicken you."

"I know, my dear. It's not your fault. It's the fault of the villagers who held you captive your whole life, keeping you in a gilded cave of their own making." He sighed. "Thank you for the fish. Now, if you'll excuse me, I wish to be alone. Tell Renata the fish were delicious, but I prefer them with the innards."

"I will," I replied. "I'm sorry we were late. I didn't quite get the hang of it until late in the day."

"Hrm," he said. "So, Renata is teaching you how to fish?"

"She is, and soon she'll teach me to hunt, too."

"Good, good. With Freja gone, we will need more hunters."

"She was a hunter?"

Ewig nodded. "The best. Her meat was always sliced clean through the neck, and without bruises, which I always appreciated. Bruised meat is offensive to my palette." He finished his plate and nudged it toward me. "Well, hunter. I tire of this conversation, so I bid you adieu."

I picked up the plate and turned away. "Right. Thank you again for not eating me."

Ewig curled around himself like a dog in front of a fireplace. "Think nothing of it. Now go away, before I change my mind."

# Chapter 22

When I returned to the cave from feeding Ewig, all eyes were on me for a moment, before they darted away back to their cleaning, sewing, and eating.

"I suppose you heard all of that?" I said as I walked across the bridge toward them and made my way down the stairs.

"Not every bit," Renata said. "But enough."

"And it's not hard to fill in the rest," Mari added, looking up from her sewing.

"Why is he so crabby?" I asked. "He's so ill-tempered, even when he's being nice."

Nur chuckled. "You get that way when you are old, and he is very old."

"I heard that!" Ewig blustered down the cavern walls.

"Good, you old coot!" Nur shouted.

Mari reached for a cup and Selma filled it with red liquid from a pitcher. "Ewig is harmless, but he is abrasive. That is for sure."

Fadia handed the cup to me. "Drink up, kid. You're officially one of us now."

I grabbed the cup and took a sip. It was bitter and sour in equal measure, and I knew it immediately as wine. They used it as a sacrament in church service, as we drank from the cup to signify our devotion to the dragon lords who bled for us. The church wine had less of a bite, but it left the same tingle in my mouth as it burned my throat, and I hated it.

"This is terrible," I replied, handing the cup to her.

Renata laughed. "You get used to it after a while."

I shook my head. "I don't think I'll ever get used to it."

"Well," Fadia said, "it's not like it's easy to ferment on top of a mountain. I'm doing my best."

"No, no, no," I said. "It wasn't—I'm sure it's great if you like wine. I just never have. Even when they forced it down my throat at service, I had to feign a smile once it was down my throat. After all, the last thing you wanted was a cedar who vomited up the sacrament she was a symbol for." I looked down at the cup. "Thorna loves wine, though. Bella's agnostic to it, but she'd rather have apple juice."

"How is Thorna?" Renata asked, being the only person who knew her in the encampment. "She was barely a child when I left."

"She's a little hellion. I'm sure she's going to escape before her ceding and take Bella with her. Maybe Leyhan, too—she's smarter than we ever were."

Renata sighed. "Yeah, I bought this sacrifice thing hook, line, and sinker, up until the end."

"Me too," I replied. "Now, I can see how stupid it was, but it's like Sister Milka kept me in a fog."

"That woman," Nur growled. "She was old when I was young. I can't imagine how ancient she is now."

"I hope she got the crow's feet that she always complained that I had." Mari touched the sides of her face. "She never thought I was good enough for Ewig. I heard her a bunch of times say that she hoped he wouldn't reject me and blight the town. That would finally put me in my place—she must have really hated me to wish the town harm for my insolence."

Fadia placed her hand on Mari's shoulder. "I think you're beautiful, little one. She found a way under all of our skins."

Mari wiped the tears from her eyes. "I don't know why she can still get to me, even a decade hence. I feel so silly."

"We're all just tired," Renata said, before turning to me. "Come on. Let's go to bed. We'll feel better in the morning."

Fadia groaned and stood up. "She's right. This is way past our bedtime." She smiled at me. "You're a terrible influence."

"I'm sorry," I replied.

"That's a joke, child," Nur said. "You're fine. It's always hard bringing a new girl into the fold. Lots of late nights until things settle down, and then, it's quiet for a while, until we do it again."

"But it's okay," Selma added, standing and wiping the last crumbs from the table. "We need a good shaking up every now and then. It's good for the soul."

Something about her words brought a chill in the air, as the cedars all looked around at each other for a long moment, before they broke it off with a fake smile and awkward laugh.

"Tomorrow you'll till the land with me," Fadia said. "Make sure to get your rest. It's much harder to work the soil than to walk through the woods and hang out by a lake."

"Hey!" Renata said with a false sense of irritation. "I don't see you complaining when your belly is full of fish and meat."

"Ladies, ladies, ladies," Selma said. "You are both valuable members of the community. Let's not split hairs."

Renata yanked me toward her. "And on that note, I'm taking this one to bed before this leads to blows."

Renata turned toward the door and led me up the hill. When we were out of earshot, she looked at my horrified expression and laughed.

"We were just playing around," Renata said. "Don't worry."

"I just never had that kind of relationship with anyone. It's so free, and loose. You all finish each other's sentences."

"That's what happens when you're stuck with the same group of people for years on end. You become a kind of family."

"It's nice. I like it. They're much nicer than Ewig."

"Yeah, about him. You have to understand something about him. He's old."

"Yes, you all said that already."

"No, you're not understanding. Nur is old. Fadia is old. But Ewig is ancient. He was old when the first of us was sacrificed. He was old when the world was young, and he will be here after we are all gone. It doesn't matter if he saves us now, he will still have to watch us die in the end." Renata sighed. "It's weighed on him more and more over time. I wouldn't wish that on anyone. It's enough to make even the kindest person hard, and he wasn't kind, even when he was nice."

"I never thought about it that way."

"Just remember this. He didn't kill you. Even though he knows you'll eventually have to die; even though the town gave you to him as an offering, he didn't kill you. In one way, he might not be the nicest creature in the world, but in another, he's much nicer than anyone from town, because he saved you while they let you march to your death."

# Chapter 23

I thought when my head hit the pillow I would be out, like the previous night. However, even though my body was tired, my mind raced all night, and while I slept in fits and starts, I was wide awake before the sun rose the next morning.

Renata's words flitted through my mind all night. How Ewig had seen everyone he ever loved die, and how he would watch all of us die before the end, and he would be around long after even the youngest of our town's children's children's children were old and shriveled. Would he even remember us when we were gone for so long? Why would he help us, if we were alive only a fraction of a second in his life?

Did he have some sort of plan for us? Or was he really just content curling up in his cave as we milled around? What purpose did we serve, if not to die? Surely it had to be more than to live in a cave scavenging all day. There had to be some greater purpose for this new lease on life...or was it just selfish and naïve to think that I had some great purpose?

It had been beaten into my head my whole life that I was special—that my life meant something, and to realize that wasn't true unmoored me in a way I didn't expect. Suddenly, I was not special at all, but just a small piece of an uncaring universe. Had I not walked up the volcano that night, nothing would have changed. If I had never been born, nothing would change. If I escaped, nothing would have changed.

Ewig was the key to it all. If he hadn't chosen this volcano, then the whole course of my life, of all the girls' lives, would be completely different. Maybe we would have found the gems hidden in the mine ourselves and been richer for it. Or maybe it would have set off a new war.

I crawled out of bed in the wee hours of the morning, before the moon had sunk below the mountains, and made my way down to the cave opening. It was completely dark out, and I feared turning on a light in the cavern, just in case somebody was hunting or fishing late in the night.

I scrambled to find a pot in the dark and filled it with water before placing it onto the steam to warm. The water streaming through the cave was already warm, so it didn't take long for it to steam. There was a small outcropping of dandelions outside of the cave opening, and I picked several for tea. I cleaned the roots and placed them, root, stem, and leaf, into the cup.

When the pot boiled, I poured in the water and let it steep for a long time. It wasn't quite what my mother made me when I was sick, but it still reminded me of home. I hated that I missed the place, but that didn't stop the fact that my heart kept reaching out for my bed, and my mother.

I longed for the caress of Leyhan's hands around my shoulders, and for the snack cakes the baker made special for me every Saturday. They weren't kind to me, except in the small moments, but those were what I longed for—the Sunday sermons where people would praise me for my sacrifice, and the times when people broke their guard and treated me to a smile.

What were they doing right now? How were they dealing with my death? What would they do if they found out I was still alive? Renata's family took years to move on from her death, even though they didn't talk about it, but Mari's seemed not to miss a beat, birthing another child and throwing all their love into her, surrounded by the opulence her sacrifice afforded them.

Part of me wanted my mother to move on, but another, darker part of me hoped my death would eat away at her for years, haunting even her deathbed.

There would be a wonderful parade for me this weekend, to commemorate my life, and to bury an effigy of me in the church grounds, surrounded by the other sacrifices. It was one of the holiest places in the whole city, except there were no girls there, and they hadn't even been sacrificed as everyone believed.

Everything they thought was a lie. What good could come from a lie?

I sat in the dark, drinking my tea, ruminating on all of it, as I listened to the soft growl of Ewig's snores lightly drift through the room. I don't know what possessed me to stand and climb up the stairs, or make my way across the rope bridge to Ewig's lair, but before long I found myself drifting through the corridors of the cave between us. My gait was easy and relaxed, so unlike the last time I walked down these halls.

Perhaps it was that Ewig was asleep, and in his sleep, he sounded like a cat purring, but it was the first time my heart didn't race, and my stomach didn't drop at the thought of him.

The fire warming him had faded and now, only a small section of the great blaze burned, filling the top of the room with smoke that slowly sifted through the cracks.

He looked less frightening in his sleep. He was still enormous, of course, but his stomach rose and fell gently, like any other animal I had ever met, and his head curled around his feet, like the stray dogs that slept near Leyhan's house.

I took a sip of tea as I watched his leg twitch, and he moaned as if he were in the throes of a pleasant dream. He didn't look like much of a savior or a villain in that moment. No, he looked as vulnerable and exposed as I ever had.

It was a lot we villagers placed on Ewig's shoulders. In exchange for our praise and worship, he was meant to protect our city and bring us bountiful harvests, along with fostering prosperity throughout the land by keeping the volcano at bay.

It always seemed so possible when the great dragon lord was a mythical figure, but now, looking at him, twitching his leg like he was running in his sleep, it was comical to put so much on one being's shoulders, even if that being was a great and terrible dragon.

# Chapter 24

I meant to only sit next to Ewig for a moment, but the next thing I knew I was lying on the ground, stretched out across the warm cave floor. My eyes fluttered open, and I reached for my tea.

*How long had I been asleep?*

"Did you sleep well?" Ewig growled at me, his eyes piercing through me.

"Uhhh," I replied, scooting back. Suddenly, the fear that had vanished last night came flooding back. "I'm sorry for disturbing you."

He shook his head. "It wasn't a bother. You are a quiet sleeper, which I appreciate, but what brought you here, to my chamber, in the first place?" He sniffed the air. "And what is that charming smell? Dandelion tea? My, I haven't had that in a long time."

"Would you like some?" I asked, sliding it toward him.

"That actually sounds lovely." He blew fire out of his nostril. Not a lot of it. Only a small, precise stream that fit inside the cup perfectly. "Ingrid used to come here and have tea with me, before she left."

"That must have been hard for you," I said.

"It has all been hard." He gently licked the tip of the cup. "Do you mind?"

His eyes moved from the cup to me, and I realized he wanted me to pour it on his tongue. "Oh, no problem."

"Thank you," he replied. "I don't want to destroy this lovely mug. It's hard to find metal in these woods."

I moved forward and grabbed the cup. Ewig opened his mouth, and I was stunned to witness rows and rows of enormous, jagged teeth as big as my leg, and thick as my whole body. His tongue laid lazily at the base of his mouth, but with a simple flick he could have wrapped me up in it and swallowed me down his gullet. A bitter, acrid smell of sulfur mixed with a light moan as Ewig pushed himself up and licked his lips.

"Yes, that is the stuff. Where did you learn to brew tea like that?"

I smiled at him. "My mother used to make it for me when I was sick."

"She must have been lovely."

I looked up at him. "Well, she let me come to this cave to be eaten by you, so I guess lovely is relative."

"Yes." His eyes met mine. "It must be hard to be a cedar, knowing your only purpose is to die by my hand, or teeth, as the case may be."

"But you didn't kill me. You didn't kill any of us. Why?"

He sighed. "Murder is really the rest of my family's domain. They came up with this ridiculous sacrificial ritual and sullied the good name of dragonkind. You know, there was a time when we worked closely with humans, instead of lording our power over them."

"Was that before—when the gods—you know—"

"Before we killed the gods?" He nodded. "Yes. I almost think having something on this planet more powerful than us kept us in check. It gave us a reason to partner with the humans to take them down. But after the humans were defeated, and we were able to defeat the gods by ourselves—I think it went to my brother and sister's heads, and humanity, well humanity has always wanted to worship something, and we were the next best thing."

"They slaughter their sacrifices, then?"

"As far as I know, yes, but they don't even enjoy it. Human meat is lean and stringy. They do it for power." Ewig sighed. "I'm not sure if they give dragons a bad name, or I give them a good one...not that I am anything special."

"You are special," I said, sliding forward without even thinking about it. "You could have killed us all, but instead you let us live with you, and you protect us."

"I don't know about all that. I simply hate the tradition of slaughtering children. I am perfectly happy with fish, and the occasional boar. You humans are too gamey for me."

I could tell something else was going on below the surface, but I was scared to pry much deeper for fear of angering Ewig and causing him to fly off the handle. However, I couldn't stop myself as the words came through. "Did you love her? The first one you let stay here? Is that why you let her stay?"

Ewig groaned. "That is a personal question. Were you not taught manners?"

"I was," I replied. "I was taught much by the nuns, but they also taught me to die, and do so gracefully, so it's hard to distinguish between right and wrong with their teachings." I sighed. "Everything I've ever known has blown up in my face, and I have no idea what to do with my life."

"I'm sure Renata and the others will teach you. They are very knowledgeable, and they have all been through this. There are no better teachers than them."

"Even the ones that left?"

A wince of pain shot across Ewig's lips. "I fear you are getting too close to my heart, little one. I hear the others coming in for breakfast, and I think it is time you go."

I grabbed the cup and nodded to him. "If that is what you wish."

"She was a lot like you," Ewig said. "The founder's daughter...Sharonda. It wasn't like what it is now. There was no great ceremony. She had no preparation. She was scared, and alone, and betrayed by those that loved her best. However, she went to her death with grace, and when I looked into her eyes...I simply couldn't eat her." He blinked, and when his eyes opened again, they were watery. "She looked me right in the eyes, and for the first time, I did not see fear in a human's eyes. You asked if I loved her, and yes. I think I did. I think I have loved each of you, in your way. Some more than others, and some different than others, but I loved her. When she died...I thought I would never recover. Sharona built this with me. She welcomed every girl for three generations. This wouldn't exist without her."

"She sounds like a lovely woman." I thought for a moment. "I wish I was like her."

"You are. She was strong, Gilda. Every one of you is stronger than you can ever imagine. You came to your death willingly. Trust me when I say that is the most noble thing a human can do, and I have watched the bravest men I've ever known run like cowards from it. There is a great power inside of you, and you will be okay."

"Thank you."

I heard a cough behind me and turned to see Selma in the door. "Why didn't you ever tell me that story?"

"I suppose I thought it might make you like me." He blinked the tears out of his eyes. "Now go, fetch my breakfast. I'm hungry."

"Come on, Gilda," Selma said. "Let's get you ready."

# Chapter 25

Two hours into tilling the garden with Fadia and I was ready to keel over. By the time it was midday, I was sucking wind so hard I could barely hear Fadia talk to me over my gasping breath.

"Nobody ever believes me that the garden is hard work," Fadia said as she took refuge behind a shady rock. "But making food isn't as easy as killing it."

She reached forward and grabbed a handful of cherry tomatoes as the sun blazed high overhead. When she leaned back, she beckoned me over to her. When I sat down, it was as if the entire morning's worth caught up to me at once, tensing all my muscles and causing them to seize up. Fadia reached over and massaged my neck with one hand, while plopping several tomatoes into my hand with the other.

"Eat something and you'll feel better," she said.

I stuffed all the tomatoes in my mouth at once, and then went back for another round. "Thank you."

"Don't eat them all," she replied. "That's all of our food, remember."

I took another deep gasp and fell backward. "You're right. I'm used to getting as much as I wanted."

She laughed. "I remember those days. You learn to get by with less over time."

"Or you leave, right?" I asked.

She stumbled and hesitated as she tried to stammer out an answer. "Right, yes, you're right."

"Something wrong?" I asked.

She shook her head. "No, it's just that we don't normally have girls leaving, unless they die, of course."

"But most of the beds upstairs are empty."

She nodded. "Yes, I know, but it's not normal. Sharonda taught us to stick together."

"So you knew her?" I asked. "The first girl to be sacrificed? There's almost nothing on her in the archives."

Fadia nodded. "Yes. She was very old by the time I came here, and frail, but I knew her. They don't like talking about her, except as some sort of mythic figure who bravely walked to her death, as an ideal for us to aspire to...to not cause trouble. That wasn't the Sharonda I knew at all."

"What was she like?"

"She was funny, for one. Funnier than she had any right to be, given her father, who was strict and hard. He didn't listen to anyone or anything that didn't agree with him. She, on the other hand, was kind, and tolerant. Mostly, she was the sun we all revolved around. When she died—I didn't know how we would survive, but we did, for a time—until the Exodus."

"The Exodus?"

"I shouldn't—" She bowed her head for a moment, and then pushed herself up. "Enough talk. This garden isn't going to till itself, and we have to till it before we plant the fall crops." She looked over at me when she was erect again. "After all, Nur has you tomorrow, so I have to get my use out of you now. After all, I don't think you'll be back down here for a while."

She was right. I hated farming. Of course, I wouldn't ever tell her that. Instead, I just smiled and grabbed the till. After wiping the sweat from my brow, I got back down to work, even though I hated every minute of it.

Renata passed by in the early afternoon with a bucket full of fish and two rabbits. I longed to get back out into the forest so that she could show me how to snare a trap, and even use a bow to hunt. Fadia's work was beautiful, and important, but it wasn't for me.

"Did you always love working the land?" I asked Fadia as the sun fell on the day and we cleaned ourselves up.

"Absolutely not. I was much like Renata when I was younger. It wasn't until I aged that I understood the beauty of creating something from nothing, instead of snuffing out a life. There's a lot of anger inside of you right now. I know, because it was in me, too, and there's nothing wrong with that, but it takes all types to make the world turn, and there is always another way to feed yourself. You can do it with anger, or with peace."

I laughed. "There's nothing peaceful about this farming life or fighting the ground to exert your will on it."

My laughter caused Fadia to laugh. When she was done, she stepped forward toward me. "Well, that's my secret. I still have a lot of anger in here, even now. It's just buried deep down below the other stuff."

# Chapter 26

I thought my body was sore the other days I woke in the caves, but it was nothing compared to the morning after I worked with Fadia. I had aches in muscles I didn't even know I had, and every time I so much as twitched, the pain made me want to scream in pain.

"Let's go, Gilda." I turned to see Nur sitting on the bed next to me. "I already started breakfast, but we have a big day in front of us."

"Uhhh, just five more minutes." I winced as I turned over, and the pain shot from my shoulder through to the other side of my body.

Nur lurched forward and pulled the blanket from my weak, frail fingers. Even if every knuckle didn't shake with pain and exhaustion, I would have not been able to match Nur's power.

Reluctantly, I slid my legs off the bed, and struggled to pull myself to the water to brush my teeth and wash my face. Yesterday, the warm water shocked me awake, but today my lids were still heavy after splashing myself.

When I turned around, Nur had her arms crossed, looking at me with pity. "Have you had a bath yet?"

I went to shake my head, but even twisting my neck slightly was too much for me, so I just let out a low groan to indicate I hadn't. "Not since the ceding."

"Well, then. Let me show you the best part of living in a volcano." She turned to the girls, who were all in different states of waking up. "Breakfast is in the pot. Nothing fancy. Just oatmeal with raisins. You can serve yourself. Don't be animals. Clean up after yourself while I tend to this one."

Instead of heading down to the main cave, she led me further up the cliffside. The path narrowed with every step I took, until we slid along the edge, one foot carefully placed in front of the next. I thought there was no way that wherever she was taking me would be worth the danger, but then we turned into another cave, and found a series of bubbling hot springs.

Nur shed her clothes and stepped into one at the far end of the room. "I find this one is good for aches and pains. However, Renata is very fond of the one in front of you."

Nur turned away while I undressed, but I had been stripping in front of Sister Milka for years, so I had very little shame in front of women. I found a thick bar of soap in a bucket and brought it over to one of the pools. I had taken lots of hot baths in my life, but this was something else entirely. I thought I would burn entirely if I kept my foot in the pool, but Nur's confidence gave me the strength to continue into the scalding water.

It didn't take long for the tightness of my body to settle, and soon I was able to move my arms around my head enough to clean my hair and body of the dirt from the last few days.

"It's nice, isn't it?" Nur said as she dipped her head back into the pool to wet her hair.

"Very nice," I replied. "I feel like a new woman."

Nur chuckled. "Well, you have become one. Burned in fire and risen like a phoenix from the ashes. Now, you get to decide who this new woman will become, and what she stands for."

I washed the soap out of my hair and rose from the water to join Nur in her pool. It wasn't nearly as hot as the one I started with, and I preferred it to the scalding temperature of my first pool.

"How did you decide?" I asked. "That you wanted to be a cook, I mean?"

"When I came, there were many more women, you know. This place used to be bustling before—" Her voice trailed off, but I knew she was talking about the Exodus. "Everybody else had their assignments, and the girl who handled the cooking had died, so I decided to fill in, and I liked it well enough."

"The girls that left. You're talking about the Exodus, right?"

"How did you know that word?" She shook her head. "It doesn't matter. Yes, that is what we call it."

"What was the Exodus?" I asked. I hadn't brought it up with Fadia when she talked about it, but I couldn't deny my interest any longer.

"I—I don't know if I'm ready to talk about it. The wound is still fresh." She looked at me with troubled eyes. "I know that's not what you want to hear, but I promise you'll hear about it, in time, if you decide to stay."

"I think I'm going to stay."

She smiled, but there was a great pain behind her eyes. "They all say that at first. Come talk to me in a decade, should you still be here."

I heard footsteps behind, and Mari appeared in the doorway, holding two towels. "I took the towels for washing. I thought you could use a couple more, though."

"Thank you, dear." Nur dipped below the water one more time and then rose to her feet, taking the towel from Mari's hand. "These are still so soft. I don't know how you do it."

"It's all in the looming technique."

For two people who had been living together for years, there was a stiltedness to their words, and how they moved around each other, like they were strangers playing at being friends, playing at being family, but something hung between them, unspoken and unsaid.

"Have you had breakfast?" Nur asked Mari, drying herself off.

Mari shook her head. "I realized where you were going and came up in a jiff when I realized you wouldn't have towels."

"We would have gotten along," Nur said. "But I appreciate it. Gilda, are you ready to go?"

I wasn't, but the pleasant warmth of the pool was starting to cook me alive, and my joints felt much better, so I nodded and took a towel. When we were dry and clothed, I followed Nur out to the narrow cliff and down to breakfast. By the time we arrived, the rest of the girls were already sitting down, enjoying themselves, getting ready for the day. Nur looked out at them with pride as they complimented the meal, but she didn't smile, even with her eyes. Instead, she simply went to the hearth and began to stir her pot.

"Come," Nur said, beckoning me over. "Lot of work to do today."

# Chapter 27

I followed Nur around for the rest of the morning, as she carefully pulled the remaining meat off the bones of the fish and rabbit we had last night and threw them into a pot to boil. Then, she led me down to Fadia's garden, where she spent a long time choosing the freshest ingredients for her stew.

"Could you just pick some already?" Fadia said, grouchy at the intrusion into her space. "I'm busy out here."

"Patience," Nur said. "I have to find the ones that speak to me."

"This isn't church, Nur," Fadia grumbled. "They're plants. They don't speak."

"To you, maybe. But they speak to me."

"She's crazy." Fadia turned her attention to me. "The last thing she needs is to have somebody else to infect."

I laughed. "I like it, actually."

"You would," Fadia grumbled, and went across the farm to tend to her leeks.

It took a couple of hours for Nur to move around the farm, speaking to each plant, making notes of when certain vegetables would be ready to cook, and kicking herself when she found anything rotten.

"Do you see this here?" She said, pointing to a blackened tomato. "This is a travesty. We don't have a lot of food here, and it's our job to make use of every single piece of fruit and vegetable on this farm." She shook her head bitterly as she grabbed the tomato and tossed it over the edge of the cliff. "It's a pity."

With that, we wandered back up to the main cave and peeked at the stew she had boiling on the stove. She took a wooden spoon and stirred it briskly, before straining out the carcasses and tossing them into a bucket for disposal later. Then, she showed me how to chop the vegetables to cook best in the stew.

"Selma doesn't like big chunky potatoes, but Mari won't eat tiny ones, so we've come to an understanding of one-inch cubed potatoes. That way nobody is happy, but everybody eats."

I was surprised how diplomatic cooking really was between the cedars. It seemed that every piece of food had a laundry list of stipulations based on the dietary preferences of each girl. Fadia didn't like tomatoes because they burned her stomach, and Renata hated cilantro, while Mari and Selma loved it, which meant we had to chop it on the side of any dish we made. Renata loved spice, as did Nur, but the other girls didn't, which meant we could only use a few peppers in any stew, and then ground the rest into a powder for the two of them to use.

Nur's skill was not only in making delicious food, but in being a diplomat who could unite the various tastes of the women in the cave into one cohesive meal that would satisfy everyone.

"After years living together," she told me as she threw some more salt into the stew, "dinner is the only time we can put away our differences and be a family. The dynamic is always unstable at best, and frenetic at worst as the different personalities vie for having things their own way."

"I saw that Renata and Fadia have a kind of love-hate relationship with each other."

Nur laughed. "Yes, they each think the other has the easier job. Renata because she is jealous Fadia does not have to travel for hours to find food, and Fadia because Renata does not have to break her back tilling and working the earth."

"And what about you? Is anyone jealous of you?"

"They all are, dear, and we are all jealous of each other." She pointed to the far end of the cave, where Mari and Selma were busy sewing and gossiping together. "Mari has no taste, but she is a whiz with a thimble and string. Selma can cut hair and mend bones like an old master, but she has no deftness with smoked meats or canned fruits. Meanwhile, I can barely tend to a small cut, and I have no patience for the stitch. We are all jealous of each other, but also grateful that somehow, we've made a functioning society. It was easier, before, when there were more, but somehow, we survive."

*The Exodus.* It weighed on her mind as heavily as it weighed on Fadia's. I tried several times to bring it up earlier, but every time I did, her eyes faded off and she drifted away for a moment, before returning to change the topic.

"It's nice to have people you can trust."

She bit her lip when she looked at me, and then down at the cutting board. She pulled a long hair from the cutting board and held it up to me. There was no doubt it was mine.

"You need a haircut, biscuit," she said. "Luckily, Selma has you tomorrow, and she'll get you fixed up."

"When do I get to choose what I want to do?" I said. "Or will it always be decided for me?"

"Soon," she replied. "We want you to see everything that we do here, so you can appreciate it. Though, I have a feeling you've already made up your mind."

"I'm back!" Renata shouted as she walked through the door carrying a collection of fish and small fowl in her arms. I looked at her and smiled. Nur was right. If I had my druthers, I would join Renata in the woods every day. I had spent too much of my life bound to a single place. I was ready to explore. I kept that to myself, though, as I rushed over to welcome her back, and get the meat for tonight's dinner.

"Put half of that in the smoke room," Nur said. "And bring the rest to me for dinner tonight."

"Do you know where that is?" Renata asked. When I shook my head, she smiled. "I'll show you."

# Chapter 28

After Renata finished gutting the fish and deboning the fowl, she led me through a dark cave entrance to the left of Nur's makeshift stove and through a series of tight corridors until we arrived at a big, wooden door.

"It took them forever to find a suitable place for a smoker, but we need it for the harsh winters." She placed her hand on the door handle. "Watch out."

She opened the door and the smoke plumed everywhere, causing me to cough. I could barely see anything in the steam and darkness, but I could feel Renata's hand on mine, and she pulled me forward into the darkness.

Renata lit a lantern and the room illuminated in front of me, showing dozens of pieces of meat at different stages of drying and aging. Renata bent down and pulled six of her fish from her bucket, placing them on open slabs of rock around the room. When she was done, she checked the other pieces of meat, turning them over them seemingly at random.

When she was done, she turned off the light and we walked back outside. I helped her shut the door, and we snaked through the corridors until we got to the main room. The smoke followed us through the corridors, and I coughed all the way until we reached the main room.

I was soaked with sweat even though we were only in the room for a few minutes. My hair was wet and my clothes damp, as were Renata's, who shook herself off like a dog, much to Nur's dismay.

"Take that animal behavior outside!" Nur shouted. "And take your little protégé with you!"

Renata giggled as she wrapped her fingers around mine and led me out into the cool, evening breeze.

"I need a towel," I said as I sat down next to her on the edge of the cliff overlooking the whole forest below us.

"I think we can air dry. Don't you?" she said. "It's so nice out."

The cold wind made me shiver, and my clothing wasn't helping matters. Mari's clothes were thick, which held in the heat at the best of times, but they also sopped up the wet, making my hands and feet shiver, and my teeth chatter. Still, I was new, and Renata was the best friend I had in this strange place, so I just nodded. I had fifteen years of Sister Milka's lessons rattling through my head, telling me not to rock the boat, and I wasn't ready to go against them...at least not yet.

"That's...fine." I choked back my cold. "It's a nice...night."

"It's so nice out. I love this time of year. It's just crisp enough to keep your senses sharp, but not too cold that it freezes your bones."

"I can't imagine ever loving this time of year," I replied. "I have always hated it. The wind always carried with it the memories of cedars we had lost before."

"But we haven't lost them." Renata threw her hands wide. "They've been here this whole time, and you found them."

This was it. This was as good a time as any to ask about the girl's leaving. "Not all of them though. A lot of them left during the Exodus, didn't they?"

Renata's eyes narrowed. "Fadia and Nur have big mouths."

"In fairness, you were the first person to say something about it. They just gave it a name."

"It's not something that's easy to talk about," Renata said. "I'm sure they told you they weren't ready to discuss it."

I nodded. "They did."

"Well, I'm not either and I hope you will respect that." She looked up at my hair. "Nur is right. It's really time to get your hair cut. Out in the forest, that much hair is a liability."

"Does that mean you're taking me back into the woods again?" I asked excitedly, thinking I might have ruined everything by asking her about the Exodus.

"Soon," she replied. "Selma has you tomorrow, and then Mari. After that, you'll be back with me. By that time, your boots should be ready." Renata pulled the hair behind my ear.

"I'm not taking you back into the woods with that hair, though."

I smiled. "I'll get it cut tomorrow, for sure."

"What style do you want?"

"I was thinking about a bob, maybe? Sister Milka never let me even entertain the idea...but I've always wanted short hair. Something completely different from this mop on my head."

Renata nodded. "That's what I did, too." Her hair was not short anymore. She had it shoulder-length, and it was usually pulled back in a ponytail when she came back from the woods. However, now she had it pulled down, free.

"Maybe I'll shave it all off."

Renata laughed. "Selma will kill you if you ask her that." She placed her hand on the lower part of my ear, close enough that her thumb brushed my chin. "I think you would look pretty if you cut it right here."

I swallowed hard. "Then maybe that's what I'll do."

# Chapter 29

I watched the sun fall over the horizon before walking to bed, buzzing with anticipation. I couldn't wait to share my new hair with Renata tomorrow when she got back from hunting. If she thought my hair would look good chopped to my chin, then that was what I was going to do, and the next morning I sprung from my bed before anyone but Nur and nearly ran down to breakfast.

"You look spry this morning," Nur said as she ladled a serving of sticky oatmeal into a bowl for me. "Does that mean you finally feel good enough to clean tonight?"

I had cleaned the first night I came to the cave, but the last two nights I was so sore and achy that Renata and Nur gave me a reprieve, but it wouldn't last forever, and I didn't want it to last forever. I wanted to pull my weight, just like all the other girls.

"Of course," I replied. "I am hanging out with Selma all day, so I should have plenty of time to clean and not be achy by the end of the day."

"Selma, huh?" She brought the bowl of oatmeal over to me. "Does that mean you picked a haircut?"

I nodded, taking a big heaping spoonful of oatmeal and munching on it. "I'm going to get it really short, like to the bottom of my chin short."

"You're going to feel ten pounds lighter." She took my hair into her fingers. "Your hair is fine. It will make good thread for Mari." She turned to the stove and picked up a heaping bowl of fish heads and guts, turning to me with them. "I was supposed to give this to Ewig, but since you're up, can you do it when you're done? I need to get busy with supper."

"Of course!"

I couldn't believe the joy that went through my body when I agreed to feed Ewig. Even a couple nights ago, seeing him filled me with nothing but fear. Now, I was eager, even gleeful to see him. I didn't even wait to finish my breakfast before I left. I scooped up my bowl and Ewig's plate in my hand and balanced them carefully.

I made my way up the stairs and across the rope bridge with more grace than I had managed the past few days, and down the corridors to Ewig's room. The fire was out in front of him, but he still laid curled up around its ashes. When I entered the room, he had stretched across the whole of the cavern, which caused me to gasp at the sheer size of the enormous creature. Save for the first night, he had always worked to stay small around me, something I appreciated, as his size was wholly frightening.

"Good morning, little one," he said to me with a sheepish grin. "Do you have any gizzards for me this morning?"

I looked into the plate that I had been avoiding since it was placed in my hand. The heads and guts from the animals didn't sit well on my eyes, and my stomach wretched at the sight of them.

"Not sure," I said, tossing the plate down and cradling my oatmeal in my hands, now too disgusted to eat it. "I didn't want to touch it to find out."

"It's not so bad as all that," Ewig said, snaking toward it. "Who knows, you might even like it if you tried it. I'm willing to share."

"No, thank you," I said. "I won't try to get you to eat my breakfast, and you don't try to get me to eat yours, okay?"

"You couldn't pay me to eat oatmeal." He took some of the guts and swallowed them down his throat. "Bland and disgusting."

"I quite like it," I replied, stuffing another spoonful into my mouth.

"Liar."

"I'm not lying. Of course, that's what somebody was lying to you would say. So, I guess you could just trust me when I talk to you."

"And do you trust me, Gilda?"

"I trust you enough that I keep coming here, don't I?"

"That you do."

"And I haven't left yet," I said. "Not like those girls with the Exodus."

He growled heartily, giving a stronger reaction than even Renata. "Don't talk about that with me. It was a travesty and I care not to relive it."

I shrugged. "I'm not surprised you don't want to talk about it. Nobody does."

"It was a dark day in our collective history. I'm not surprised."

My eyes narrowed at him. "Have you told them not to say anything?"

His eyes narrowed, as they only did when he was upset with me. "Is this why you came today? To interrogate me?"

"No," I replied. "I was just making idle conversation."

"There is nothing idle about this conversation. It is kinetic and aggressive. And here I thought you might have come to wish me well tonight. How disappointing."

"And what is tonight?" I said, and then I remembered. It had been three days since the ceding. Ewig was due to leave his cave and make a speech to the town, thanking them for their gift. It was a tradition, and I forgot it in the hustle and bustle of the last few days. "Oh, right."

"Yes," he replied. "It is my least favorite part of this whole ceding rigmarole. Even more so than having another of you to care for." He finished his plate and licked it clean before nudging it over to me. "Take this back to Nu and ask her for gizzards and hearts next time. I like those best."

I grabbed the plate and rose from the ground. "I will." I went to walk away, then I turned back to him. "Good luck tonight, for what it's worth."

"Not much," he replied. "But thank you all the same."

# Chapter 30

Selma and Mari had a comfortable rhythm as they worked together on the far end of the cave. They didn't talk much, but they sometimes found themselves engaged with idle chatter. Usually, though, they were lost in their own thoughts, humming to themselves, as Selma cut my hair and Mari sewed one thing or another, often moving between her spindle, loom, and thread. Nur had gone to the garden to pick some food for dinner and needed to walk to the base of the mountain for some spices, so she would be gone for most of the morning.

"Were you always a seamstress?" I asked as Selma went about cutting my hair. "Sister Milka tried to get me to learn, but I have stupid fingers."

Mari thought for a moment. "That's interesting, since your mother was a tailor. Did she not teach you how to sew, or your father, the cobble—oh, right. He left."

"Yeah," I said, sadly. "He didn't have much time to teach me anything, and Mom—well, she didn't like doing much once we came into money."

"My gods," Selma said. "That sounds just like my parents. Everyone told me how my dad and mom were the best bakers in town, but I never saw them make a single, solitary thing after I was born."

"And it wasn't much better even after you were gone," Mari said. "They got so fat."

I laughed, and they laughed. It was effortless, and loud, so unlike how they taught me to laugh as a child. There was no refinement here, even between the two most demure people in the bunch of cedars.

When it was calm again and the silence started to overwhelm us, I spoke again. "Have you ever thought about going back? Not for real, but just to poke your head out and see how they are?"

"Oh, yes." Mari hopped up and spun around. "I know it's horrible. They tried to kill me, and I've been trying to wash it away for many years, but—well, sometimes I think the reason I didn't leave with the others is because I always thought I would be able to go back one day."

Selma replied like she had heard it before, and with grace through her bitterness. "But you would never do that to us, Mari, right?"

"Of course not." Mari placed her hands on her lap, atop a piece of cloth she was weaving into a shirt. "I would never turn on you. If the past year taught you nothing, it has to have shown you that."

"You have proven yourself in every respect. We all have. And the ingrates who—well, the gods will come for them."

Mari swiped at the air. "Don't say such things, Selma. You know he can hear everything."

"It's just an expression," Selma smiled. "I have no allegiance to those old, dead, fuddy duddy gods, and Ewig knows that."

Mari placed a hand on her chest. "Still, it's not right, after all he's given us, to evoke their names."

Selma stopped disagreeing and returned to chopping my hair. There was a wistful, remorseful energy in the air as they worked, every few minutes looking over at each other, and then back at their work, without saying anything.

"I'm giving you bangs," Selma said at one time. "I think they will help frame your face."

"Okay," I replied. I never much liked my forehead, but Sister Milka never let me cut one hair on my head. "So, you are a healer?"

"I used to be. There's not much use for healing with just the few of us left, so I do odd jobs, filling in wherever needed. I make bowls and cut hair. Fortunately, most of the girls are set in their ways, and don't work well with others."

"And she has fat fingers, which makes her impossible at sewing," Mari said with a smile. "She's good company, though."

Selma blew the hair out of my face. "There, I think we're done."

Selma walked around the back of the cave and pulled a shard of broken glass from the ground. She brushed it off and handed it to me. I moved it around my head, marveling at the shortness of my hair, or how much younger I looked than even my fifteen years with the hair gone from my head.

I craned my neck to the ground to see all my hair in a heap under me. I shook my head from one side to the other, and the hair that remained smacked into my face on either side. I laughed in joy as I stood up, nearly hopping with excitement.

"I love it. I love it so much!" I said, grabbing Selma with both hands. "Thank you! I never knew I could love something so much as a haircut."

"You shouldn't jump up and down," Selma said. "I still have a pair of scissors in my hand."

"And thank you," Mari said, dropping to her knees. "I'm running out of mending thread. This will help."

Selma placed the scissors behind her, and we all helped Mari gather the hair and place it in a box near the rest of her things. When we were done, Selma turned to me.

"Can I tell you a secret?" she asked me in hushed tones, even though Mari could hear every word.

"Of course," I replied.

"Mari and I...every five years we sneak into Ewig's cave to get a glimpse of the village again."

"Selma!" Mari shouted. "Don't."

"Oh please," she replied. "They all know. They don't approve, but they won't stop us either, if you want to come."

I was conflicted, but I couldn't deny that I desperately wanted to see my family again, just one last time, so I nodded.

"Absolutely. I do."

# Chapter 31

I ate dinner with unbridled anticipation, trying my hardest not to shovel food into my mouth just to get through it to Ewig's speech. I didn't know how much I desperately desired to see my mother and Leyhan, along with Thorna and Bella, even if it was from a chasm away.

I finished my meal before the others, and went to clean my plate, careful to scrape all the scraps into their appropriate buckets, and then prepared a meal for Ewig, that Nur would deliver after we were done. Then, Selma would find me and take me to the spot where they would watch the proclamation.

"Come with me," I heard behind me.

I turned to see Renata smiling behind me. "I have to clean dinner. I'm not even half done yet."

"Do it later," she replied, holding out her hand. "They'll understand."

I looked behind her, to see the miffed expressions on both Nur and Fadia's face as I moved from the wash basin. They didn't seem the understanding type, and if I went with her, I might miss the procession.

I moved my eyes from Nur's fury to Mari's consternation, looking for some guidance, but finding none. "Why don't you help me, and then we'll be done in half the time, and I can join you then?"

Renata snarled at my practicality but agreed. This had been her job for five years, and she had gotten very good at it, clearing the table and washing the dishes with a speed I couldn't muster and a mastery I couldn't touch, at least not yet. She must have been excited, because I watched her grab the plate from under Selma's nose as she went to grab a final bite of salad and slide a half-eaten plate from Nur's gluttonous fork.

"Good?" she asked, when we were done. Behind her, the whole of the dais narrowed their eyes at her. However, they didn't say anything about it. Mari simply stood up and grabbed the plate for Ewig.

"Don't be long, ladies," she said as she disappeared.

"Especially tonight," Selma replied, as Fadia and Nur found their way out of the cave and up to bed.

Renata grabbed my hand and pulled me out of the cave, and up the volcano, past the ambling Nur and Fadia, fat with food, and through the short impasse up to the baths.

"I already know about this place," I said as she moved past the pools toward a crack in the rock along the back door I hadn't seen the last time I washed myself.

"That's not what I want to show you."

She squeezed herself through the crack and beckoned me to follow. A blast of muggy heat slapped me across the face when I did, and I gasped on the suffocating hot slamming me from above.

"It's just a little further. I promise it's worth it."

She rubbed my back and smiled at me in a way that it was impossible not to believe her. In that moment, I would have followed her to the end of the world.

Renata climbed up the rough, rocky slope in front of us, and I followed carefully behind. Before long, the slope broke into the cool night air as it clashed with the heat of the caldera below.

We had made it to the tip of the volcano, and below us, the bubbling lava churned and mixed, as steam spun into the air in spiraling spindles. Renata grabbed my hand and squeezed it tightly.

"It's beautiful, isn't it?"

My heart leapt in my chest as I looked down at the molten hot magma below us. I always knew we lived next to an active volcano but seeing the proof of it sent a shiver up my spine. Ewig's most important job was calming the volcano below us and keeping it dormant generation after generation. If it were to ever anger and bubble over, it could destroy our poor village in no time.

"Yes, it's beautiful, but I think we should get back," I said, turning toward the rocky slope that led to the steamy pools under us.

"Not yet," Renata said, pulling me around the lip of the caldera. "I haven't shown you the best part."

I wanted to turn away from her, but I couldn't let her alone in such a dangerous place, so I followed as she ran around the edge of the caldera. On one side of us, the bubbling caldera called to us, and on the other, the darkness of the night called out from the edge of the cliff, begging for us to join it.

We ran in the middle, between fear and panic, until we reached a small outcropping filled with tilled dirt, and beyond it, the dots of light from the village lit up the darkness.

"This is where Ewig buries the dead of us," she said. "All the way back to the beginning, so we can look out on the town that abandoned us and be welcomed into the great beyond forever."

Only four headstones adorned the outcropping, which meant that, with twenty cedars having been sacrificed since Ewig took up residence in the volcano, and five living in the caves, eleven cedars must have left during the Exodus. *What could have happened to drive so many cedars away at once?*

"Come over here," Renata said, beckoning me to the edge of the volcano.

As I stepped through the graves, careful not to disturb them, the town lights glittered and twinkled in the dusk over the edge of the caldera. Down there, my mother, Leyhan, the cedars, the whole town prepared for the proclamation. I saw some of their torches working their way through the sinewy streets.

"I come here sometimes, in the day, or at night when I can't sleep, to watch the city go about their business, ignorant to the truth inside their comforting lies."

"I thought you hated them."

"I do," she replied, walking up to me. "And I miss them. Two things can be true at the same time. They broke my heart every day of my life, and yet, it was the only town my heart ever knew, and sometimes it calls to me still." She took a deep breath, unaffected by the heat that plumed from the caldera behind us. "Can you imagine what they would do to us if they found out the truth?"

I thought about it for a second. "I think some of them would be happy we were alive at all."

"For a time," she said. "But soon enough, they would hate that we lied to them. They would hate Ewig, and that vitriol would transfer to us, even though we are really only pawns in their game."

"We could leave. You can leave whenever you want."

"And if we left, we would have to lie about who we were every day of our lives. No, even though it is between a rock and a hard place, at least here, we are as free as we would ever be."

She turned to me. "I wanted to show you this, to remind you how many people would hate us if they found out the truth, so that when you go with Selma and Mari tonight, and you look at their pained faces, your heart didn't break too much."

My eyes dropped. "You knew I was going with them?"

She laughed. "Of course. They are terrible liars, and even worse sneaks. There is no shame in pining for your past, but just remember this is your future."

There had always been a lightness in her voice when she talked to me, but that vanished in her last words, replaced with a hollow, dark, threatening tone. As she said them, she squeezed my hand tightly, until I winced in pain.

"Ow, you're hurting me."

"Sorry." She let my hand go and rubbed her own. "Sometimes I don't know my own strength." She turned back to the caldera. "Come on, let's get you back before Mari and Selma start to ask questions."

# Chapter 32

Renata said her goodnights to me and sojourned to bed. Fadia and Nur were already asleep, with Fadia snoring as she was prone to do. As the person who slept closest to her, I was all too familiar with her snoring on the nights when I had trouble sleeping, and she was in rare form tonight.

"Just remember, those people all sent you to your death," Renata said, grabbing the wall of the cave. "No matter how much they cry and how miserable their faces are, they still watched you walk up that cliff like a prisoner."

I looked into her pained eyes for a long moment. "I'm sorry I didn't try to save you."

She placed her hands on my cheeks. "The only two people in the whole world I don't blame are you and Thorna." She kissed me on the forehead. "Have fun tonight, but make sure you remain hidden."

With that, she walked into the cave to bed. I watched her wash her face for a moment before starting down the cliff. When I reached the main cave opening, I heard Mari and Selma laughing together, but as I approached, their voices grew silent. It wasn't until they saw me turn the corner that they let out a sigh of relief.

"You scared us," Mari said, hand on her chest.

"I thought you were Fadia, or Renata," Selma said, pouring red wine into a metal tin. "Bunch of wet blankets."

"I don't know about that. They all know what you do," I replied. "Or at least Renata does, and since she's only been to one ceding, and it was hers, I have to think she heard it from somebody else. Heck, I'll bet Ewig knows too, and they haven't tried to stop you."

Selma tipped the tin cup back and finished the cup, then slammed it on the table. "They're still fuddy duddies. Come on. It's about to start. We were about to head out without you."

"I'm glad you didn't," I replied.

Selma grunted at me and then led the pack of us up the stairs and across the rope bridge. It was harder to make our way in the dark of the moonlight, and even harder when the moonlight fell away in the tight corridors of the cavern.

"You know," I whispered as we walked, "I thought I saw your face in the darkness during the last ceding, when Ewig blew a great burst of fire into the air before he concluded the proclamation, but I thought it was just my eyes playing tricks on me."

"I told you not to get so close," Selma growled at Mari.

"I know, but I just...I wanted to see them," Mari said. "I'll stay back further this time. I promise."

Selma didn't say anything, but she let out a sigh that let me know she didn't believe Mari but continued on regardless. We reached Ewig's lair, and for the first time he was not curled up inside of it. Without the towering titan, I realized how enormous the room was. It always looked small and confining when the great dragon was present, but now the massive chasm seemed to extend upward into infinity.

"Crap," Selma growled. "We're late."

She skittered to the corridor, and I heard the faint sounds of Ewig's deep growl through the cave.

"Thank you," his voice echoed as we neared. "For your continued strengthening of our bond. It has been my great honor to preside over your bounty for these past hundred years, and with your sacrifice, I look forward to another half decade of peace."

Mari pulled me to the ground as we crawled forward. The light of the fires from the town illuminated the great dragon's shadow against the dark sky. The citizens were quite a bit below him, on the other side of the path, and I couldn't see them. It was easy to see why Mari would crawl forward.

As Ewig took a breath, I slid forward on my stomach, my eyes trying to find the tip of the ledge, so I could see my mother and the others. It was the only time I would see them for five years, at least, and though I would meet Thorna again if she made it to her ceding, who knew what would happen in five years' time? My mother might be dead, and maybe Thorna would have truly escaped.

"In payment for your cedar," Ewig continued. "I shall make sure the volcano remains dormant for another five years hence and deliver a bounty for your town that rivals the riches of the capitol."

I had to see them, which meant moving closer. As I slid forward on my belly, I felt Selma's hand on my leg yanking me back. I turned to see her glowering at me, but I couldn't quite see over the edge of the ledge, so I kicked off Selma's hand and continued forward until I nearly clipped the tip of Ewig's tail.

I still wasn't able to see the town over the cusp of the ledge but couldn't risk moving forward and having the great dragon's tail swipe me, so I pushed up to my knees. I heard Mari and Selma whisper-screaming at me, but I couldn't stop myself. I wouldn't see them for another half decade, and I had to get one last glimpse of them.

My eyes broke the edge of the cliff, and I spotted them, standing there. Leyhan had a black eye and a fat lip. What had they done to my poor, sweet boy?

Thorna and Bella stood in front of the others, as was custom. They didn't cry, and simply looked at the great dragon, understanding their fate, but not the truth. My mother stood behind them, crying into a handkerchief, while Sister Milka's stoic face glared forward, rock solid.

"In a final show of the great bond between us, I will light the sky on fire," Ewig said. "And I invite you to douse your torches and be lit only by the fire from my breath, as it kisses your face and shows my gratitude to you, my chosen people."

One by one the lights went out until the entire town was dark, and then, in a great show of brilliance, Ewig lit the sky with a thousand different colors. I lost myself in them for a moment, until Selma slammed her hand again into my leg, and I realized that the fire did not only illuminate Ewig but had fallen on my face as well. I dropped to the ground and skittered back to the safety of my sisters, but for a moment, just a single moment, I swore that Leyhan's eyes met with mine, and there was a glint of recognition in them as a smile rose on his face.

# Chapter 33

"That was really stupid!" Selma shouted when we were back in the hollow of our part of the cave. "What were you thinking?!"

"I'm sorry. I'm sorry. I just—I needed to see them." I turned to Mari. "You know what I mean."

"You must really be an idiot!" Selma continued. "I even told you what Mari did to warn you against doing the same stupid thing, and yet you couldn't stop yourself, could you? Gods, you are such a moron."

"Hey!" Mari shouted. "It's been a long time since your ceding, but I still remember how it felt to give up everything you ever knew, and I know how hard it was for Gilda, too."

"Don't you think it's hard for me?" Selma said. "Don't you think I want to see if my mother is still out there, looking up to find me somehow, by some miracle?" She stomped across the rope bridge, wobbling it too much for me to get a good grip, until she spun in the middle of it. "Why do you think I started going to the proclamation in the first place?"

Selma's voice cracked, and she started to cry, heaving her back against the rope and causing it to sway violently. Mari rushed toward her.

"Hey." Mari's voice was soft and sweet. "It's okay. It's going to be okay. We're all just freaking out." Mari turned to me. "Nobody saw you, did they?"

My mind flashed to Leyhan's eyes. They went wide with excitement when they connected with mine. I swore there was a hint of recognition on them, but that couldn't be true, right? There was no way he could see me from across the great chasm, hidden behind Ewig's great body.

"No, I don't—no. There's no way."

Mari nodded. "See, it's all right, Selma. It's okay."

"It's just—since the Exodus." Her chest heaved as she took fast, excited breaths. "I can't..."

"Shh, shh, shh," Mari said, cradling Selma tightly into her breast. "It's going to be okay."

*Exodus.* There was that word again. It touched every one of the girls down to their core, and yet they wouldn't talk about it. Now, maybe Selma would, if I framed it properly and took advantage of her weakness. I opened my mouth to ask her about it, but before I could there was a great grumbling from the other end of the cave, as the light of Ewig's fire kissed the edges of the cave.

"Oh girls," Ewig's deep voice said. "Could I see you for a moment?"

"What do we do?" Selma whispered. "I can't have him send me away. I can't survive out there with you."

"And before you think that was a request," Ewig added, "it was not. Get in here, now."

I turned from the rope bridge and waited for the others to join me. We clasped hands and walked down the corridor together. Our breaths were bated, as we neared the entrance to Ewig's lair, which looked so much smaller now that he was again standing tall inside of it.

"I couldn't help but hear your conversation," he said. "I don't have to tell you how dangerous it is for you to keep tempting fate, do I, Selma?"

She stepped forward, shaking, but as she didn't let go of our hands, she pulled us forward with her. "No, great dragon lord. I am a-a-aware of how dangerous it is."

"Good," Ewig said. "I feel like we have the same conversation every five years. Perhaps if you love your village so much, this is not the right place for you."

She shook her head. "No, please. I don't want to leave the cave. I like it here."

"Do you?" Ewig cocked his head, but his voice didn't raise. He was most understanding, which was unlike him in our last interactions. "Because you keep doing these things that endanger our safety."

"We're sorry," Mari said. "This was my fault. I shouldn't have told Gilda."

"No, you shouldn't have, Mari," Ewig replied. "I thought you would know better. If I recall, this last kerfuffle was caused by one of your—"

"I know!" Mari shouted. "I know I've done wrong before, but it wasn't me this time. It was all the new girl."

Ewig's eyes shifted to me. "Ah, yes. You seem to have a mischievous side, don't you?"

"Have I? I've tried to be good." I swallowed hard. "Haven't I been good?"

"This is your third day here, and you've already endangered us once. Do you feel that is something a good person would do?"

I shook my head. "No, but I didn't mean to—I will try to be better."

Ewig sighed. "I know Renata told you that you can leave if you aren't comfortable here. I am not a warden, and you are not a prisoner, but if you are to remain here, then you must do things my way, understood?"

"Yes, sir." I said.

Ewig's eyes shifted to Mari. "I thought better of you."

"I don't know why," Mari said. "You barely know me. In the ten years I've been here, we've barely talked more than a dozen times."

Ewig thought for a second, introspectively. "Unfortunately, it is hard for me to make my way through to you, Mari. You know that. However, you are always welcome to come here and speak to me. That you have not chosen to do so except when forced is as much a reflection of you than it is of me."

Mari didn't say anything. She just began to cry, which caused Ewig's face to drop. "We will both try to be better, okay?"

Mari nodded. "Okay. Thank you, dragon lord."

"Good." Ewig yawned, unhinging his jaw and exposing a dozen rows of teeth to us. "Now, this has taken a lot out of me, and I need my sleep. If you wouldn't mind, I need to sleep now."

"Yes, sir," I replied. "Thank you for not killing us or burning us alive."

"You don't have to say that every time," Ewig said, softly. "Did you get what you wanted tonight, Gilda? Did you see your family?"

"I did."

"And was it everything you ever expected?"

I sighed. "No. I wanted it to be closure, for me to say goodbye, but there was nothing, except hollowness and sadness where I thought my release would be."

"It is not easy, what you have done." Ewig rolled over. "But I hope you will settle into it soon enough or choose to leave if you cannot."

"Is that what you want?" I asked. "Is what you want for me to remain, or would you rather me go?"

"Either is fine with me, but right now, I want you to go away, so I can sleep."

He closed his eyes, and the conversation was over. I looked over to Selma and Mari, who didn't have another word to say either. Instead, we walked off, out of the room, and off to bed, with the unspoken agreement we would never speak about it again to anyone outside of the three of us.

# Chapter 34

I woke the next morning with a quiet dread filling my belly. What if Leyhan had seen me, or gods forbid somebody else in the village? Would they think it was a trick of the mind, or could they possibly believe I was still alive? I kept pushing the thought away, trying to convince myself there was no way they could have seen me, and they even if they did, it wouldn't matter, but the niggling thought ate at the back of my brain as I got ready for the day, swamping me with every false smile and fake pleasantry I gave to the other cedars as we went about our morning routine.

I made it down to breakfast after a long steam, ready for my day with Mari, learning how to sew, but when I saw her at the table, she turned from me, toward Selma, who dropped her eyes rather than look at me.

"Come on," Renata said, a bow slung over her shoulder. She slammed a pair of new boots into my chest. "You're with me today."

This was what I wanted, to be with Renata, and yet, it felt hollow and wrong. "But—what about Mari?"

Renata looked back at her. "She says you have fat fingers, and could never learn how to sew. So, you're stuck with me today. Put on your shoes and eat fast. We have a long day ahead of us."

That was the story she gave Renata, but I wondered if the truth was that she couldn't look at me after last night; if the guilt of it ate away at her like it ate away at me. I wanted to talk with her, but would have to wait until we were alone, or at least until she was only with Selma, before I confronted her.

Nur had baked bread, and pulled jam preserves out of her storeroom deep within the volcano and paired it with eggs that Renata collected from a nest the previous day. Eggs were a luxury, I found, as we didn't keep chickens like in the village.

"We're going to start with an easy snare," Renata said when we finally got into the woods where she equipped a quiver of arrows and a pair of long knives. "If you can set this trap, you'll never be hungry for long."

She knelt in front of a young sapling and bent it to the ground before tying it off. Then, she removed a taut piece of rope and tied it in a loop, before securing it to the tree. When she moved back from it, the sapling wiggled slightly, and then stayed put.

"When an animal walks the loop, the snare catches and snaps its neck. Quick and painless."

The brush rustled as Renata placed a piece of carrot inside the loop. She pushed back quietly behind a tree, pulling me behind her. I poked my head back to see a little brown jackrabbit emerge. It pulled up on its hind legs and sniffed the air before catching the scent of the carrot.

It moved forward quietly and quickly, and I turned my head before hearing the snap, either from the branch or the rabbit's neck, I couldn't tell which.

"That was quick," Renata said with a smile. "Usually it takes hours and I have to set a dozen traps to catch one of these little guys."

I stepped forward to see the light fade from the rabbit eyes. Renata was right. There seemed to be no pain, but that didn't stop my heart from breaking any more. It was different from the fish, somehow. Maybe because I saw it before we captured it.

"How can you do that to something so innocent?" I said it without accusation. "I don't know if I could ever do that."

"I think about who I'm doing it for. I'm doing it to feed you, along with Fadia, Nur, Mari, Selma, and Ewig. We eat what we catch, and I don't catch any more than we need." She stopped for a moment. "It's them, or us, and I will do anything to protect all of you." She placed the rabbit around her shoulder. "If you can't do this, then tell me now. I'm sure Fadia can use help in the garden, and Nur said you were very helpful to her in the kitchen, too."

I thought for a moment. *I couldn't do this, could I?* But I didn't want to be stuck back at home either. If I had to do a job, the one I wanted gave me freedom to move around the woods, and the lake, while everything else kept me glued to the volcano. I had spent too many moons stuck in one place.

"N-no. I think I can do it."

Renata smiled. "I was hoping you would say that, because we can really use another hunter. Now, it's your turn."

"C-c-can I watch you do it again?"

Renata shook her head. "No. If you're going to be a hunter, then you have to learn to hunt. I'm here to teach." She pulled the rope from her pocket and handed it to me. "But you have to learn if you want to keep coming out with me."

Sadly, I was a natural at setting snares. Unlike fishing, which took strength and finesse, the snares only took meticulous surgical skills, along with deft hands, and that suited me just fine. It was lucky that none of the other snares tripped while we walked to the lake, so I didn't have to see the horrible fruits of my labor, and we spent the rest of the day fishing.

"I think you might have found your calling," Renata said as she pulled in another catch. "Not fishing, of course. You're right terrible at that, but the snares took me weeks to master, and you did it in one day."

"Good." I flicked my wrist, casting the line out into the vast lake and starting to reel it in. "I like it out here."

"Me too," Renata said. "So much more peaceful than the caves, and so much better than the village."

"You really think that? I mean, we had everything for a short time. Even though we were being fed like a lamb for slaughter, you don't at least miss the luxury of it, even a little?"

Renata shook her head. "No way. Back home, I was nothing but a stuck pig. Here, I'm a hunter. I have freedom. I can go anywhere. If I chose, I could go beyond the lake. I could write my own ticket."

"But you wouldn't do that, because of the girls."

"And Ewig."

"Right, and Ewig."

When my line pulled up nothing, Renata looked at the sky. "I think we've done all we can do today. Let's try the traps and see if you caught anything. Then, we'll start back."

# Chapter 35

The first traps didn't yield any results, but they held all day, which Renata said was a good thing.

"We'll check them tomorrow morning, and hope anything that they catch isn't too decomposed by then, or that some other predator hasn't gotten to them yet."

The third trap was another story. We arrived to see that dead carcass of a vole hanging in the middle of a thatch clearing. It hadn't been disturbed by anything, and hung listless, its neck broken and eyes glassy.

Tears filled my eyes as I moved forward toward it. "It's so small."

The light streaming through from the midday sun illuminated the vole from behind making it glow an ethereal light, like an angel ascending into the Heavens to take its place among the stars. It would still be alive if not for me, but now it hung limp and loose. Did it have a family waiting for it to return with food? Would the little animal's death cause a chain reaction that led to the death of many other little animals in the forest?

Renata must have seen the trepidation in my face, because when she turned to me after cutting down the vole, her face was softer than I had seen it in days.

"You did good today, and you can't take it too hard. As terrible as this is to hear, these little critters were bred to be food for bigger predators. If we didn't kill it, something else would."

"That's a horrible thing to say," I replied, choking on my sadness.

"The world is horrible," she replied, her face hardening with every word. "And you have to do what you must to survive. It's the circle of life. One day we will return to dirt and become food to nurture the plants these critters eat, and the world will keep turning."

Renata used to be the type who would cry when somebody killed a spider or stepped on an ant. She was loving and kind until the day of her ceding. How did she become a stone-cold killer?

"Do you remember when that rat scurried through the schoolhouse?"

"Which time?"

I connected with her eyes. "The time when Sister Milka grabbed it by the tail and slammed it on the corner of her desk, killing it in front of us. We all heard its neck snap."

She thought for a moment. "Oh yeah."

"You cried for two days," I said to her.

She shook her head. "I was young, and naïve, just as you are now." I raised my voice to object, but she stayed my mouth. "And I know what you're going to say, but trust me, you are still so very naïve."

"That's not what I was going to say," I lied. "I was going to say that it wasn't so long ago that little girl was standing in front of me. What happened to turn her into this cold-blooded killer?"

Her brow narrowed, and she stepped toward me. "I am NOT a killer." Her voice was forceful, and a terrible meanness carried under it. "How dare yo—"

In the distance, a twig snapped, and Renata spun on her heels. She pulled the knife from her belt and pressed her finger to her lips. I heard the steps in the silence between us, crunching the leaves under them, stepping lightly, but too hard to conceal itself completely.

Was it another small critter that would be our dinner, or something more dangerous? My heart fluttered in my chest as Renata pulled me to the ground and we moved behind a bush big enough to conceal us both.

She stowed her knife and pulled the bow from behind her back, nocking an arrow into it and leveling the weapon at the rustling brush in front of us. The bushes shook and rustled with a heft much bigger than the small animal that we had seen yesterday. Maybe it was a bobcat, or a small bear, but whatever it was made me nervous.

We waited another moment, and a small doe popped out of the brush and hopped toward us. Renata growled, stood, and shot the deer in the neck. It cried out in pain as blood soaked the light brown and white spots that coated its body.

When it fell to the ground and gasped for its last breath, Renata laughed.

"Wonderful," she said. "We'll eat for a month on this catch."

My eyes focused on the deer's eyes. It had just been alive, and now, moments later, it was dead at our hands. It was the last straw. "I don't think I can do this. I have to—" My breath heaved in my chest and came out in quick heaves. I tried to calm my nerves, but I could only grasp for air as I fell to my knees.

"Easy, Gilda," Renata said. "It's okay. Nothing can hurt you here."

"That's not—not what I'm afraid of. I'm af—afraid—" I couldn't keep talking as I gasped for air. My hands found the ground, and I clutched the earth with all my might, digging my fingers tightly into the wet topsoil.

Renata dropped down and rubbed my back. "Calm yourself. It's okay. It's okay. Close your eyes and count to five, slowly."

I did as she asked. Five one thousand, four one thousand, three one thousand, two one thousand, one one thousand. When I finished, my heart stopped thumping in my head and my breathing had returned to some semblance of normal.

"Better?" Renata asked.

"No," I said. "I thought I could do this, but I can't—just look at that poor little thing."

The tears fell from my eyes, and Renata took me tightly into her chest. "It's okay. It's okay."

There was another silence, and in that silence, I heard a familiar voice, one that I hadn't heard in a long time.

"Gilda," it said. "It really is you. I knew it."

My eyes rose to find Leyhan smiling at me, and that is the moment I knew Renata was wrong. Nothing would be okay ever again.

# Chapter 36

*I couldn't believe it.* Leyhan stood in front of me, smiling, just like he had a thousand times before. He didn't waste any time sliding down to his knees and grabbing my hands, pulling me from Renata's gaze.

"Are you really alive?" He said with a giant smile on his face. "Or is my mind playing tricks on me?"

"Uhhh," my eyes bounced from Renata to Leyhan, whose eye was still swollen, and lip fat as I saw it last night. "I'm—alive."

"I knew it!" he shouted. "I just knew you weren't dead."

"How?" I asked.

"I saw your face behind Ewig last night, just as you told me about with Mari last time, when Renata—" His brow furrowed, and he turned to Renata, his brain suddenly making the connection for him. "Oh my gods, Renata? What are you doing here?"

She stood and backed up from him. "I could ask you the same question."

"After I saw Gilda's face, I set out, that very minute, to find a way into the mountain, up the forbidden mountain path. I knew nobody came to this side, and thought that maybe, just maybe there would be a way to climb up to find you.

That's when I heard your voice. I couldn't believe it. I thought I was hearing things. I thought this whole thing was a fool's errand, but now—" he caressed my face with his hand, and another shock electrified my body, "—now, it's like I can fly."

Renata had enough of this line of questioning and moved forward to tower over us. "Have you told anybody where you were going?"

He shook his head. "No, they would have tried to stop me. I just left."

"Good, that's very good." There was an ominous tone to her voice. "And you want to get up the mountain?"

"I wanted to find Gilda, and I want to know what's going on here. How many of you are there?"

Renata smiled. "I'll tell you, if you help us get this doe up to our cave. You look like a strong boy, it shouldn't take long at all."

He thought for a second. "I will help you, as long as you promise to tell me the truth."

Renata placed her hand on the dagger secured on her hip. "Cute to believe you are in a position to negotiate here, but yes, I will tell you everything, if you simply help us."

Leyhan gave me a final look and then nodded. "Then lead the way."

He went to pick up the doe, a small thing, barely out of being a fawn, as I leaned into Renata. "What are you going to do with him?"

"Relax," she replied. "I told you it would all be okay, and I meant it. We'll bring him to the girls, and they'll know what to do. Trust me."

And I wanted to, but the first rule they told me when I first arrived is that I couldn't tell anyone I was still alive, and while I hadn't broken that promise, somebody had found out anyway. Still, Renata was in power here. She had the weapons, and the know-how. All I had was the will to live, and the will to keep Leyhan safe.

Renata took point in front of Leyhan and I as we walked back to the volcano. Even a rookie like myself couldn't get lost with it in front of us. Every so often, she would look back at us and grin, as we walked forward, both of us in a daze at seeing the other one.

"What have you been doing here?" Leyhan said. "Why didn't you come back to the village if you've been alive this whole time?"

"They wanted me dead," I replied. "Renata, and—well, she took care of me. Showed me how to hunt, kept me alive. She's the only person I knew who wasn't trying to kill me." I caught the hurt in Leyhan's eyes as they dropped from me. "Except for you, of course."

"I would have taken on the whole of the mayor's legion if you let me." He favored his right side, and the weight of the doe made him wince with every step on his left foot. "You know that."

"What did they do to you?"

"Nothing," he said, trying to brush it off, but I wouldn't let it go, and it must have come across in my face. "They made an example of me. What do you think? They strapped me to the whipping post in the middle of town and showed the whole town what happened when somebody lied to protect the cedars—when they even thought of upending tradition."

"I'm sorry." I touched his back and he winced again. "Oh no, I'm so sorry."

"It's still raw," he said. "Thorna spoke up for me, but it didn't matter. They didn't listen to her. They don't actually want you cedars to open your mouth and express an opinion, just be their symbol."

"Yes," I replied. "I remember."

We made idle chit-chat for the rest of the way back to the cave, him asking questions, and me deflecting at Renata's behest. When we passed Fadia's gardens, I was happy to see she was not there to complicate matters.

"Wow, you have a farm, too?"

"Yes," Renata said. "We have built much here. We are more than just blood for the fodder."

It was another thirty minutes up the mountain to the cave, and Leyhan was completely out of energy by the time we reached the entrance, where all four of the other women stared at us when we entered without saying a word, fear written on their face.

"Put it over there," she said.

Leyhan looked around at all the faces in the room, and then at me, before finally settling on Renata. "Fine, but then you'll tell me exactly what's going on."

"As we agreed."

Leyhan hobbled the last few feet to the stove and tossed the doe off his back and onto the ground, where it landed in a thud. He was sucking wind hard as he turned back to us and dropped to a knee, too tired to fight against Renata, who rushed forward and slammed her fist into his temple, knocking him unconscious.

"Come on, girls," she said, turning to us. "Help me with him."

# Chapter 37

"What did you just do?" I shouted, rushing toward Leyhan's unconscious body, before Fadia and Selma leapt from their chairs to hold me back. "Let go of me!"

"You don't understand. I had to." Renata turned to Selma. "Take Nur. Tie him to one of the beds until we can figure out what to do with him." Then, her eyes fell to Fadia. "Meanwhile, you and Mari keep her calm. I have to go talk to Ewig."

Selma and Nur moved in sync, each picking up Leyhan by an arm and carrying him out of the room. I kicked and screamed, but Mari and Fadia just held me harder, until I had no energy left and couldn't fight them.

"It's a shame," Mari said. "He looks just like his father."

"His grandfather, too," Fadia added. "I would have very much liked to sleep with him, in my younger days."

"Gross!" Mari replied, laughing lightly.

"What? I'm a woman, and I like men. Do you know the last time I saw one? My gods, how it makes my blood boil."

"Yes," Mari said lowly. "I know exactly how long it's been."

Fadia sighed and her eyes dropped. "Of course you do."

They moved me to a chair, and sat on either side of me, gripping my hands tightly. "You're hurting me."

"That's not our intention," Mari said, but her grip didn't abate. "But you're not thinking clearly."

"And you are?" I tried fruitlessly to struggle against them. "You just watched Renata punch my friend unconscious, and now you're tying him up! This is crazy!"

"Hey!" Fadia shouted back, matching my anger with her own righteous fury. "Don't you think we know that?"

"I thought you were my friends." Tears fell down my eyes. "I thought you were my family, but you're nothing but common thugs."

"That's not fair," Mari said. "We're looking out for our own. Renata says we have to look out for each other first and foremost."

"We have to make sure our secret stays safe," Fadia added, nervously.

"And what are you going to do?" I said. "Cut out his tongue. Kill him?" At that last question, they became very jittery, and couldn't meet my eyes. "Oh my god. You are going to kill him, aren't you?"

"We don't know!" Mari shouted. "This is complicated. If the town found out about us, do you know what they would do?"

"Nothing good," Fadia added. "That's for sure. Who knows? They might even kill us."

"And so you'll kill somebody else just to keep your secret? That's not right!"

"None of this is right!" Fadia shouted. "None of this was supposed to happen. Not again, not so soon."

"Wait, what do you mean? Again?" I asked. "This happened before?"

Before they could answer, Renata's voice boomed from the rope bridge. "Yes, it did. Two years ago, Mari's brother came looking for her." Renata made her way down the stairs. I remembered that Mari's brother went missing, and was never found, but we assumed he found another town, or was lost in the woods like so many others. "When he found us...well, he came looking for her, but whatever joy he found reuniting with his sister was replaced with vitriol and anger when he found all of us living in secret under his nose."

"We tried to reason with him," Mari said. "We really did, but everything I said made him angrier and angrier. He vowed to bring the whole town down on us, on Ewig."

Fadia sighed. "We took a vote. The five of us ended up on one side, and Freja and the other cedars ended up on the other, saying we should let him go and trust the townspeople to be merciful."

"I have never known them to be merciful," Renata said. "Ever. So, I did what needed to be done. I made the hard decision."

"Wait...are you saying you voted to kill your own brother?" My eyes found Mari's face, but her eyes fell from mine, so they moved on to find Renata's. "And you followed through and killed him?"

"There was no other choice."

"She's right," Nur said, walking inside. "She had to protect us."

"By killing somebody?"

"They sent us to our death," Selma said, walking in behind them. "How is this any different?"

"It doesn't matter if it's different. Killing people is wrong. They're wrong for doing it, and so are you."

"Yes," Renata said. "That is what Freja and the others said. They left that night, after it happened, cursing us to our fates." She stepped forward toward me. "If Leyhan is allowed to return, he will destroy everything we built."

"If what you've built is so precarious that one person finding out threatens it, then maybe it deserves to be destroyed."

"And what if that leads to our death?" Mari asked, lightening her grip. "They will hate us if they learn the truth. My brother proved that."

"They should hate you," I replied. "You killed one of theirs."

"They will hate Ewig. They will come for him. He doesn't deserve this. He only wanted to be left alone."

"Don't put your guilt on me." Tears streamed down my face. "I love him. I love Leyhan," I gasped. "That's the first time I have said that out loud, but it's true. I loved him since the first time I met him."

"And I loved my brother," Mari said. "But I made a promise."

"So did you," Renata said.

"I didn't know that promise would involve murder!"

"Neither did I, but we do what must be done." Renata looked around the room. "Are we in agreement?"

The rest of the women, the women who until just minutes ago I thought were my family, nodded solemnly, a betrayal that had only been matched by my mother—hrm, perhaps they were more like my family than I realized.

"Good," she said. "Then I will lead him out to the water and do the deed. It's no different from bleeding a rabbit."

"No!" I shouted. "You can't! I don't agree!"

"You've been outvoted!" Renata shouted. "It must be done."

She was no better than the villagers. At the first sign of distress, she chose to sacrifice my friend, my love, rather than risk her life, her safety, her survival.

"This isn't right," I growled.

"Your opinion is noted, and unfortunate." Renata said. "Mari, take her to Ewig. He'll decide what to do with her. The rest of you, get the prisoner ready for transport."

"Why don't you decide my fate?" I asked. "You seem to be good at that."

"You are his cedar," Renata replied. "If he wants to kill you, he's the only one who can make that call."

I didn't fight Mari as she dragged me to my feet or moved me across the rope bridge. I had already been marched to the great dragon lord once in my life, a sacrifice for an ignoble people. As we turned into the cave, I wished that I died that night.

At least then Leyhan would be safe.

# Chapter 38

I was foolish to think things could be different here. Everywhere was the same. People trying to control you, justifying violence, lying to me...lying to themselves. I wanted to cry, but I didn't have any tears left.

"We're not the bad guys," Mari said, squeezing me in a death grip. "We didn't have a choice."

"You can keep telling yourself that," I replied. "I assume that this schism between you and the others is what caused the Exodus? The thing you guys wouldn't tell me about?"

"Yes," she replied. "It hurts my heart every day to think of them leaving."

"Then you just proved you did have a choice. Your brother didn't have a choice. Leyhan doesn't have a choice. I don't have a choice, but you had a choice. You could have left. You could have stopped Renata."

"I'm a tailor, Gilda. I'm not built for fighting."

"And Renata wasn't built for killing, but she took to it easily enough. You were right not to tell me. I would have left that very minute."

"If we had more time, you would have understood."

The heat from Ewig's breath blew onto my face the closer I got to his lair. The hot air, which so recently suffocated me, was little more than an annoyance now. Mari stopped marching forward a dozen feet from where the cave broke open. She was still scared of him. I was walking to certain doom, and she was the one scared.

"I forgive you," I said as she let my arm free. "Not for killing your brother, or Leyhan, but for whatever happens to me now, I forgive you."

"You shouldn't."

"I know," I replied. "But I still do. That's my choice. What you do is yours, and we both have to live with it."

I didn't turn back to her, but I heard the sobbing coming from her as I stepped defiantly forward to meet my destiny. Ewig was not curled up in front of his fire but standing in front of the other exit to the cave, so that I couldn't run from him. But even if I got free, where would I go?

"Ah, little one. You have caused quite a bit of trouble, haven't you?"

"I didn't mean to—"

"We never mean to do anything, but our consequences have actions. If Anjari did not kill my sister, then we never would have turned against the gods and taken their place. I would never have come here to protect this town, and this volcano, and you would not be here today."

"You're not protecting anything," I said. "You are a joke. This whole place is a joke."

"It is a cruel joke if it is one, but why do you spew venom on me? Did I not save your life not four days ago? Was it not you who were noticed by the boy, and you that led him here?"

"I wish you had killed me that night," I said.

He growled loudly. "I did say that one day you might regret me sparing your life. I thought it would happen when you were old and brittle, but I did tell you it would happen, eventually."

"Please," I fell to the ground. "Great dragon lord. Please, save my love. Save Leyhan."

His eyes narrowed. "I can see how much you care for the boy, but he threatens our way of life."

"Well, your way of life is terrible, then. If it can't take even one person finding you without falling apart, if it descends into murder at the drop of a hat, it's nowhere I wish to live."

"Do we not have the right to defend ourselves?"

"From what? From the threat of persecution? You don't even know what they will say if you save Leyhan's life and he tells them."

"I know Renata will be convicted of the murder of Mari's brother and hang. Do I not have a responsibility to her?"

"She committed a crime. Leyhan has done nothing. Please, let me go save him and fix this. Please, I'll do anything. Please. We'll go away. We'll run. You'll never see us again. Please, please, please."

"Do you really think you can keep that promise? That Leyhan won't immediately run back to your people and tell them everything; that they won't come after us if he tells them everything?"

I pushed myself to stand and wiped my tears. "No, I can't, but you should do it anyway. Otherwise, you're nothing but a coward."

He snorted fire from his breath. "You know not to whom you speak."

"I know exactly who I speak to. The Great Dragon Lord, Ewig. I have been devoted to you my whole life. The stories they tell about your bravery, and yet, now I see the truth. You are nothing but a weakling, curled up in his cave, hoping nobody finds out what you really are. I can't believe I was ever scared of you."

"I am no coward!" Ewig boomed, his neck shooting toward me. He gnashed his teeth inches from my face, but I didn't move.

"Prove it. Let me go save my love, and deal with the consequences should I succeed. Maybe I will fail, and get there too late, and Renata will kill me for you, or maybe I will find a way to beat her. Either way, it's out of your hands. And isn't that what you really want, to be absolved of any decision?"

He eyed me for a long moment, a moment I didn't have as each one that ticked by was one fewer that I had to save Leyhan. However, in the end, he pulled back.

"Very well, child. Know that you hold your village's fate in your hands. If they come for me, I will destroy them without a second thought. However, I will let you take your fate into your own hands."

"How noble of you." Sarcasm oozed from every word.

He raised his claw and pointed to the wall of his cave, closest to his right. "Behind these rocks is a fissure that will lead you outside into the night. If you take it now, you might even save him. I had better never see you again."

I didn't say thank you. I was sick of thanking people for the simple right to live. They weren't noble for allowing me to take my fate in my own hands, and so I stayed silent as I ran to the crack and pushed myself inside, disappearing into the darkness to save the love of my life, and one of only a few who never tried to kill me.

# Chapter 39

The sloped rock path was narrow and slippery as it led me down through the darkness, and I found myself losing my footing often. I thought the insufferable darkness would never end, but then I found a pinprick of light inside of it. I slid toward the brightness and slipped out into the grass once it engulfed me. I made it to the base of the mountain.

Ewig was true to his word, but I didn't give him much credit for it. After all, he was sending me into the lion's den, armed with nothing but my wits, and I wasn't sure I had much of them given what I was about to do. I could go back to the village, and call for help, but then Leyhan would be dead. I couldn't let that happen. He would do anything to protect me, and I needed to do the same for him.

I found the tree where Renata stored her weapons and grabbed a bow and quiver of arrows. Renata would not be in a hurry. She would not think I could escape Ewig, nor that he would let me go. I passed several of the snares I placed earlier that day, so proud to bathe in Renata's praise, before I knew the kind of person she was.

I kicked them away as I moved. Even if I couldn't save Leyhan, at least I could keep the blood of the forest animals from my hands. I weaved and ducked between the bramble and the trees, lashed over and over again by the tiny branches that acted as whips against my face, cutting my hands as I refused to stop.

I had never gotten to the lake faster, and my head throbbed with the beat of my heart when I finally found Renata on the edge of the water, holding her bow to Leyhan's head, his hand wrapped around his back in surrender.

"Get on your knees," she ordered, and he compiled.

"Just tell me you're going to take care of Gilda. I'll gladly die to save her."

Renata shook her head. "I don't have any control over what happens to her, but I'll tell you what, I think she's a coward, and if I had my druthers, I would kill her, too. She is nothing like I imagined. She'll never be able to join us, not knowing what we've done to you, and we can't let her go, either. I only hope Ewig does the noble thing and kills her."

Renata's elbow twitched, but she didn't loose her string. I couldn't wait any longer. I pulled the bow off my shoulder and placed an arrow in it.

"That's enough, Renata," I shouted, pulling it back to my ear as I stepped out from the woods. "Put down the bow."

"I'm sorry, kid, but I can't do that."

"Gilda!" Leyhan shouted. "Run!"

"You know Leyhan." I took a step toward her. "You played with him as a kid. Your families ate with ours. He's not just an animal, he's a human."

"He's one of them!" she shouted. "They are all animals. Now, put the bow down before you embarrass yourself."

Renata moved the bow toward me, and I took the opportunity to loose my arrow, which flew wide, missing completely, but giving Leyhan a perfect distraction to jump forward and knock Renata down. They tussled for a minute, before I heard Renata scream. Leyhan had driven a hunting knife deep into her shoulder.

"I'll kill you!" Leyhan screamed.

"NO!" I shouted back. "You're better than that. Let's just go." He looked over at me for a moment. "Please."

Leyhan snarled at me, and then knocked Renata across the head, knocking her out. "This is a bad idea."

"No more death," I told him as he rushed to me. "I can't have any more of it." I placed my hand in his. "Now, let's go."

# Chapter 40

We ran until we couldn't breathe and had to stop. I had no idea where we were even running to, except away from the lake and Renata, deeper and deeper into the foreboding woods. I couldn't return to the cave, and the town thought I was dead.

"We have to keep going." The din of the woods mixed with the panting of my breath, and Leyhan's wincing as he rubbed his leg.

"You need to rest. You're in no condition to run."

"She won't be out forever, and when she comes to, she'll be after us. If we can get to town then—"

"Are you crazy?" I growled. "I can't go back there. Not after everything they've done to me."

"Then what do you suggest?" he asked.

"Let's take the lake around. There must be a town somewhere that will take us in."

"They're our family, Gilda, and they believe a lie. I can't live with myself knowing they are going to keep worshipping a lying, conniving dragon."

"A dragon who let me go to rescue you," I corrected him.

"One who lied to our people for a century." He pushed himself to stand and started to hobble forward. "You can go if you want, but I have to tell them."

There was a determination in his eyes I had seen before. Renata was right. We couldn't stop him from talking without literally killing him, and I wasn't about to do that.

"They're going to hate me," I replied.

He held out his hand for me to take. "Not if you tell them the truth."

He was so confident, I believed him. I placed my hand in his and we continued on through the woods.

My gut tightened and my body tensed with every step we took toward the village. Leyhan assured me it would be okay, but what did he know? He was beaten for a lie, a small lie that ended up not hurting anyone. Ewig's lie hurt everyone and had for a hundred years.

As we walked, I told Leyhan everything I knew about the caves, Ewig, the first girls, and the Exodus. I didn't know everything, but what I didn't know I patched together with inference and guesses, smoothing over everything into a cohesive narrative, trying to weed out the truths from the lies on the fly.

We continued through the trees until they thinned into a path that led us over the mountain, canopied by the forest. The sounds of birds singing and the forest waking up echoed through the trees as we neared the town, and the light peeked through the trees welcoming me home. I wanted so badly to hate it, but I couldn't deny the butterflies fluttering in my stomach at the thought of returning to my childhood home.

"Are you ready for this?" Leyhan asked.

I kissed him softly on the lips. "Oh, you sweet boy. Absolutely not."

The world busied itself coming back alive as children bustled to school with their parents, and people went about their jobs. However, we were safely cocooned on the edge of the woods. Once I took another step, I would break from that safety and my fate would be in the hands of the town.

"Come on, then," Leyhan stepped forward, his foot breaking the safety of the woods with a confidence only a man who had never been treated as a sacrifice could.

I went to take a step forward out of the woods, but my body shook with hesitation. Leyhan was confident I would be okay, but how could he be sure?

"I knew you would come here," a familiar voice growled behind me. I turned to see Renata step out from behind a bush holding a knife. "If you do this, Ewig will burn this whole city to the ground."

"We won't live in fear anymore," Leyhan said, though his voice cracked when he spoke, belying the strength of his words.

"So unnecessarily confident." In the distance a child laughed, and Renata's ears pricked up.

"Are you sure you want to make that decision for everyone?"

"They can make that decision for themselves," I replied. "Leyhan is correct. We have no right hiding this from them. They're rational. If I lay out the case, they'll accept it. Then, you can come home. You can all come home."

"I don't want to come home!" Renata shouted. "They sent me to my death. I never want to see them again."

"Then why do you sneak up to the caldera and look down on them? Why do you stay close? Why do you not leave and start a new life somewhere else?"

"They took my life away from me...and if you don't come with me now, I will take yours from you."

"Look, Mommy!" a little girl shouted. "It's Gilda!"

I turned to see a little girl, rosy faced with curly hair, pointing at me. I recognized her as a first grader from Sister Milka's school. Her mother stared at me, mouth agape. The girl's words stopped the street cold, and they all turned to look at me.

I snapped back to Renata, who was gone, and we were in it now.

# Chapter 41

Once the initial shock of seeing me faded, the terror sunk in. People screamed "what does it mean?" and accused me of running away into the woods to avoid being a sacrifice. Two soldiers came forward and ripped me from Leyhan's arms. They separated us and led us away to the prison, where we sat for the whole day, staring at each other between steel bars.

As the sun fell, the door to the jail creaked open, and my mother shuffled into the room. Her mascara smeared her face, and she looked ten pounds lighter than I had seen her just a day before.

"My little girl." Her face beamed with joy and love for me as she pressed her hands through the bars and grabbed my cheeks. "You're alive. You're really alive, and you've come back to me."

I couldn't stop the tears from falling, even after everything she had done to me. "It's good to see you again, Mama."

"Is it true what they said? Did you run away, flee to avoid being a sacrifice?"

I shook my head. "No, Mom. That's not it at all. All the girls are alive, and Ewig is not a killer. I'm going to set them straight. You'll see."

"I don't know if you're going to get the chance, my love. The mayor aims to have a trial

in the main square, and when it concludes..."
She choked back a tear. "They plan to kill you."

"No, that can't be," I said. I was willing to die
for the truth, but not for a lie. "It's not true.
They're all up there. Ewig let me live. He let us
all live. You have to believe me."

"I do, my dear, sweet girl. But the others...I
don't know. They lived their whole life believing
one thing, and it's hard to get people to change
all at once, even if it's for the truth."

Two guards entered the room and pushed her
forward, tossing her into a cell on the other end
of the room from me.

"What are you doing to her?" I screamed.
"She had nothing to do with this!"

"Quiet!" one of the guards shouted.

"I'm so sorry," Leyhan said from the cell
across from me. "I didn't think—I thought they
would want to know the truth, but now I can
see—we should have run."

It was a small solace to be right, especially
now. By the time the guards left, I knew why
they arrested my mother. They meant to make
an example of us all—of what would happen if
we went against the will of the town. My simple
existence spat in the face of everything they
understood about the world, and it was easier to
believe a comforting lie than face the harsh, ugly
truth that they had been duped for a century.

Later in the day, the door creaked open
again. This time Thorna entered, her face dirty
and her usually white cloth pegged with mud.

She held Bella in front of her, who was equally dirty but in considerably better spirits.

"My gods," I said, rushing to the cell. "What happened?"

"People are mad," Bella said.

"They have no idea what to think, so they're lashing out. The soldiers brought us here for our protection."

"You aren't in trouble, are you?" Leyhan asked. "I couldn't live with myself if they arrested you."

"No," Thorna said. "We're fine, I think." She smiled at me. "I can't believe you're still alive. I'm so happy."

"Me too!" Bella shouted.

Thorna smiled. "I never thought you would be the one to bring this whole stupid system crumbling down."

"Me either," I replied with a grin of my own. "I guess you rubbed off on me."

The night brought a bonfire vigil, where the townspeople screamed for my head, and in the harsh light of day, the guards came to drag me out of my cell, with Leyhan and my mother close behind.

On either side of the door, citizens of the town were held back by soldiers as they clawed toward me, angry for my blood. I honestly preferred their viciousness to be public, instead of hidden behind a coy smile and banal platitudes. This was their horribleness manifested, and now it was on display for me to see.

In the town square where a party had been erected in my honor a day ago, they had built a scaffold with three nooses. The mayor and town elders sat upon a judge's tribunal behind it.

The crowd from the jail followed us to the gallows, screaming obscenities behind us. They hadn't even heard my truth and already made the decision that I was a heretic who deserved to die. Though I supposed they already decided I should die back when I was born, and if Ewig were not to kill me, they would do it themselves.

The soldiers lined us up in front of the nooses, and then turned us to face the judges. Elderman Florence looked at me with pain in her eyes. The mayor, meanwhile, had nothing but cold rage behind his, and the other two elders sported expressions somewhere in the middle. In front of them all, Sister Milka stood, eyeing me.

"Gilda, you are accused of a great crime," the mayor's voice boomed. "Perhaps the greatest crime in all of our great village. Your selfishness has unmoored us all, and we brought you here today to pass judgement on your transgressions. How do you plead?"

"Innocent!" I screamed. "How could I—you were there, at the proclamation, where Ewig gave his blessing on this town. How could I have escaped if he gave you his blessing?"

There was a murmur in the town. The simple folk of the town hadn't thought of that.

"Quiet!" The mayor slammed his fist on the ground. "We don't know what witchcraft you used to beguile the great dragon lord, but he will soon learn of your treachery, and we must show him that you do not speak for us all."

"You have soiled our good village with your heresy!" Sister Milka shouted. When her eyes leveled at mine, her face contorted. "You have damned us all!"

She lunged at me, but the guards held her back. She kicked and screamed until the mayor banged his hand on the table and called for order.

"Sister Milka, you trained this girl from the day she was born and walked with her up to the edge of the cave. How do you think she escaped? Did you aid her?"

"Of course not!" she screamed. "I take my position seriously. I am the salvation of this town, and I would never desecrate that to protect the cedars from their destiny."

"It's true!" I screamed. "She did everything right. She brought me to the volcano and watched me walk to my death. She was all too happy to watch me die. It was the great dragon lord himself that saved me."

"LIES!" Sister Milka said. "I don't know how you got away, but you lie!"

"She doesn't lie!" Leyhan screamed. "I saw five of our former cedars alive with my own eyes. They are living in the caves on the other side of the mountain!"

"You're speaking nonsense, boy!" Elderman Florence said. "Love has blinded you."

"I'm not lying! I was captured by them. They were going to kill me. Gilda saved me. She brought me back here. She agreed to tell you the truth, even though you tried to kill her, because she thought you deserved the truth."

"And what about the harvest?" Elderman Thomas, who had until this moment been completely silent. "Ewig provides for us."

"No, he doesn't!" I replied. "He is just an old shut-in living in a volcano who wants nothing to do with any of this!"

"So, Ewig lied to us?" Elderman Florence said. "My friend didn't have to die?"

"She didn't die!" I screamed. "None of them died. Five others are alive, living in the volcano right now."

"Don't believe her lies," the mayor growled. "She has bewitched our dragon lord and now tries to bewitch us all!"

"I'm not lying!" I shouted. "If you don't believe me, just follow me around the mountain, and I'll bring you right to the cave."

"What game are you playing at?" the mayor asked. "This won't save you."

"Yes, it will," Leyhan said. "Because it is the truth. Bring the whole town if you want, and we'll go to the volcano. We'll show you the way."

"Ah ha!" the mayor shouted. "So you can escape!"

"We'll be chained and can't run anyway." Leyhan said. "You lose nothing, except a day of your time. In return, you could gain freedom." Now, Leyhan turned to look at the townspeople. "We have been lied to for generations. It is time to break that cycle today, and regain the grip that Ewig has held on this town for too long."

The crowd exploded in applause, which caused the mayor to think for a moment, before nodding his head. "Very well. I suppose we can wait until tomorrow to hang you."

# Chapter 42

It took half the day to hike to the mountain path that led up to the caves. Half of the townspeople followed the cadre of guards that flanked Leyhan, my mother, Sister Milka, and I, with the mayor and eldermen behind us as we led the way. None of them had ever been to this side of the valley before, having been told it was a sacred forest only accessible to Ewig.

I could see the fear in their faces as we walked through the bushes and brambles, every step taking them further from the town than many had ever been. I remembered the feeling well, as it was the same one I harbored only days ago. It was incredible to think about how far I had come since the ceding. Back then I was a naïve girl, ready to march to my death, and now I was marching to save my life.

"There it is!" Leyhan shouted, raising the shackles he had been bound with to point his finger at it.

"Wait," I replied. There was something on the path. As we neared it the five cedars—Mari, Fadia, Nur, Selma, standing behind Renata— made themselves known, holding weapons, waiting for us a dozen steps up the mountain.

"I thought you would come with less people," Renata said as we continued toward them.

"What's the meaning of this?" the mayor stammered.

"Didn't Gilda tell you?" Mari replied. "We've been living here quite comfortably for the last century."

"Mari?" a man's voice shouted. "My dear sweet girl. Are you alive?"

"Yes, Pop, I'm alive," Mari said. "Not that it matters to you."

"Are you kidding?" another woman shouted. "If we had known—"

"You would have done what, Mom?" Selma shouted. "You sent us to our deaths!"

"But you're not dead," a shrill woman shouted. "It's a miracle."

"It's not a miracle!" Sister Milka stammered, trying to find a way forward. "It's a travesty! We have been lied to all this time! Guards! Arrest them!"

Renata stepped forward with her bow. "No, I don't think we'll be going with you today, Mayor."

The mayor scoffed. "And what will five girls do?"

He barely got the words out before the sky turned black and the sound of leathery wings cracked through the air. The clearing in front of us erupted in fire, and Ewig crashed onto the ground, screeching a terrible, thunderous bellow into the air.

"They won't do anything," Ewig growled. "But I will defend them with my life." His eyes turned to me. "I told you to stay away, child."

"This wasn't my idea," I said, holding up my chained hands.

"Yes, and now you see the truth," Ewig said. "And why we kept it hidden for so long."

"How could you do this to us?!" one townsperson screamed, breaking Ewig's gaze.

"We believed in you!" another added.

"I didn't ask for any of it!" Ewig growled. "I never cared for my family's demands but went along with it anyway. That was my fault but giving your daughters to me was yours. The edicts from my sister never said I must eat the sacrifices, just that they must be given to us every five years. Their lives are in my hands, and I chose to spare them. That is my choice, and I will protect their lives with mine, and take yours if you choose to attack."

"Then it's a war you are after?"

"No," Ewig growled. "I don't wish to kill anyone. All I ever wanted was to be left alone."

"Kill him!" a woman's voice shouted.

"Destroy him!" another screamed.

"Stop!" I screamed, ambling forward between them. "I get it, we lied to you, and it wasn't nice." I turned to the townspeople. "You feel raw about it, but you sent us to our deaths. It's a miracle we aren't dead yet, and that Ewig took pity on us, something you never did." I turned to the cedars on the mountain. "Selma was a cedar twenty-five years ago, and Ewig has returned her to us." I pointed to Nur. "And that's Nur, she was a cedar thirty-five years ago."

"That's my sister!" a woman's voice shouted.

"Hi, Hester," Nur said with a polite wave.

"And Hester," I shouted, "you now have your sister back. Isn't that a miracle?"

"Yes!" Hester shouted, her voice quaking with tears.

I spun to the crowd. "And all the others are miracles in their own right."

"What if we don't want to go back?" Renata said. "What if we can't look them in the eyes."

"Then don't go back. Or if you want to live in that cave, do it. But can we please just stop lying to each other? We can overcome this, but we can only move forward if we all agree every one of us sucked before and promise to do better in the future."

I looked Renata in the eyes as she held her shaky bow toward me. The next instant, she loosed her hand, and the arrow flew through the fire, landing at my feet.

"Your boyfriend stabbed me."

"And you tried to kill him. I think we both need to bury the hatchet, but not into each other's head if possible."

"Touche," she replied.

I turned to the cedars. "What do you say, can you admit you kind of sucked for lying about being alive?" They grumbled half-hearted yeses and I guess sos. Then, I turned to the crowd. "And can you admit you kind of really sucked for trying to feed us to a frigging dragon?" Again grumbles all around as the town came to agree they were kind of the worst. "Good. Halfhearted acceptance is better than nothing. We can work with that."

"This doesn't even begin to make up for everything we've done to each other," Renata said. The weight of the murder she caused weighed on her with each word, and while I couldn't forgive her for what she did, that was her burden to bear.

"No, but it's a start."

"And what about the dragon?" the mayor asked. "It has kept us under its thrall for a century."

"I did no such thing. I just wanted to be left alone. Now, go away before I burn you alive." He stepped through the fire toward the mayor. "Especially you. And let my friend go while you're at it. Only I get to kill her, and I say she lives, as do the others, including the boy and her mother."

"I—I think I can live with that," the mayor said.

"It is the only way you live."

# Chapter 43

The guards untied me and shakily went on their way back to town with the other villagers. Ewig laid on the fire until it dissipated before walking over to Leyhan and I.

"Are you okay?" my mom asked, grabbing my hand.

"I'm okay," I said. "Give me a minute, okay?"

She agreed and walked away, waiting for me out of hearing distance, but I doubted she would let me out of her sight for a long time.

"Flowery words," Ewig said. "I thought for sure I would have to burn them all down."

"You might yet," I said. "The mayor wasn't happy to be shown up, and I think the townspeople are still in shock. When they come back to their senses, their bitterness might take over."

"I'll be ready for them."

"And what about you?" I asked. "Are you going to leave?"

"Absolutely not. This is my home. I allow you to live here, but the volcano gives me life. When the war was over, I was quite beat-up, and this volcano fed its energy to me. In a funny way, maybe I did protect the village after all, in my way."

"You're going to have to be more involved in the town now, you know."

"Make me." He turned back to the other girls. "I think I have plenty of surrogates to work on my behalf."

"I don't think they like me very much."

He laughed. "No. I don't think either side likes you much right now, but you were able to broker whatever tentative peace we have, so they respect you at least, and I like you, for what it's worth."

"It means a lot."

Ewig nodded and floated away, leaving me face to face with Renata, who walked forward and pulled the arrow from the ground.

"Thanks for not killing me," I said.

"My aim was off," she replied. "I was going for your throat."

"Then it's a good thing you never taught me to shoot."

She smiled a little. "You didn't tell them about Mari's brother."

"And I won't," I replied, turning to Leyhan and grabbing him by the hand. "Neither of us will. We have to work together to keep peace, and that is your burden to bear." I smiled to myself. "It's funny, the only real killer here is you."

"No, it's not funny." Renata sighed loudly. "I guess I'll be seeing you around."

"You will. We have to build a new future now."

# Author's Note

I found the cover for this book many years ago, in a cover buying frenzy when I first decided to make a go of being an author, thinking "people love dragons", and I should make a dragon book. I had no idea when I would have a chance to write it, but I had the idea immediately—the story of a girl who was meant to be a sacrifice to a dragon and ended up befriending it.

Gilda is such a lovely character to write and also a great challenge. When I write my other characters, they are fighting AGAINST something. They don't want a bad thing to happen to them, but Gilda was willingly going to her death, and I had never written a character that would be so selfless. It was a challenge to get her right, and make sure she stayed consistent through the course of the story, especially when she changed over time after meeting the other cedars. It was a great joy, though, to see her change when she is given a second chance at life, and start to embrace it, until by the end she's fighting for her life instead of willingly giving it up.

It went through many iterations through the years. Gilda was once going to be part of a harem for the dragon, and the dragon was going to be a shifter. I thought about making it a paranormal romance between Gilda and Ewig, but no matter how I tried to fit them together, none of them made sense for me, for this story.

In early iterations, there were also way more cedars, like 20+, one for every five years, and I couldn't deal with that many, which is the main reason why I created the Exodus. The fact that Renata killed somebody was always there, but before the girls were all united on it, and I thought, especially for a series, having some conflict helped build out the whole world.

This all finally came together after I met an artist who I really wanted to work on this book with, and while the graphic novel fell through, it gave me the direction I wanted to take with this book. I try to grow with every series I write, and with this book, I tried to tell a very small story that focused on a character changing and growing without the fate of the Earth in the balance, though...well, wait for books 2 and 3.

Most of my books are these big grand adventures, with epic heroism and universe altering potential, but with this book I wanted to do more of a character study, like *The Void Calls Us Home*, but even more intimate. With that book, I had some big moments inside the void, but with this I wanted to keep everything small, and for it to take place over a very short period of time, also not a strength of mine.

I thought this book would be 25,000 words, and so the fact I was able to double that count by adding more very small moments made me very happy. I've never been able to do that before. It's another tool in my writer toolkit which allows me to slow down a story when previously most of my skills involved speeding a story up, not bringing it to a halt while still making it interesting (or at least I hope it was interesting).

If you follow my work, then you probably know that heterosexual relationships don't happen often in them. I thought for a while about having her fall in love with Renata, and there was a little bit of that in here during early drafts, but in the end, it made sense that she was with Leyhan, and ended up with him and Gilda together.

Originally, there was also a best friend character, too, who was named Renata, but instead I chose to combine the best friend with Leyhan, because they both served similar points in this story, of fighting against the patriarchy of the town, and it felt too much to have them both in there together, mimicking the same thing the other said. However, I loved the name Renata so much I chose to keep it around and use it for the cedar who ended up bearing her name.

I also wanted to show the relationship between Gilda and each of the cedars in detail. That was important to me, that it felt like a functional group dynamic, and you loved them. I needed you to feel for each of them before I pulled the rug out that they were as big an antagonist as this story gets, at least until the sequels.

In the next book, *The Dragon Champion,* we learn more about the girls who left during the Exodus, and the other dragons, as the town interacts with more people, and the action ramps up. I still intend to make that book a smaller exploration than you might be used to for my work, but I do hope you enjoy it.

# Also by Russell Nohelty

**THE OBSIDIAN SPINDLE SAGA**
The Sleeping Beauty
The Wicked Witch
The Fairy Queen
The Red Rider
**THE GODVERSE CHRONICLES**
And Death Followed Behind Her
And Doom Followed Behind Her
And Ruin Followed Behind Her
And Hell Followed Behind Her
And Conquest Followed Behind Them
And Darkness Followed Behind Her
And Chaos Followed Behind Them
Katrina Hates the Dead
Pixie Dust
**OTHER NOVEL WORK**
My Father Didn't Kill Himself
Sorry for Existing
Gumshoes: The Case of Madison's Father
The Invasion Saga
The Vessel
Worst Thing in the Universe
The Void Calls Us Home
The Marked Ones
**OTHER ILLUSTRATED WORK**
The Little Bird and the Little Worm
Ichabod Jones: Monster Hunter
Gherkin Boy
**www.russellnohelty.com**